Lesson Five

"Should I touch you now?" she demanded, but receiving no response, decided to do so anyway.

As the palms of her hands met the textures of his jacket, she could feel beneath it the stern presence of his spine and the graceful muscles rippling away on either side of it. She was slowly allowing her hands to inch ever so innocently around him, when she felt his grasp on her tighten.

He tenderly urged her head backward, then, bending over her, with a hunter's instinct he found her more than willing mouth with his own.

Withdrawing his lips, he murmured, "Emma . . ." As he bent down again toward her, she was hurled into a giddy spiral of delight . . .

THE KISSING LESSON

JOANNA BURGESS

A JOVE BOOK

First Jove edition published September 1981

First printing

Printed in the United States of America

Jove books are published by Jove Publications, Inc., 200 Madison Avenue, New York, NY 10016

For Harvey

Author's Note

Lest the reader be troubled by the sometimes strange admixture of dates, places, and conventions in this little tale, let him be advised that it is a work of fantasy, set in that lovely time out of time, where miracles can always be called up in the service of romance.

And since what is perfectly
possible is apparently impossible.
the impossible must be possible.

—JOHANN VON GOETHE
Elective Affinities

Chapter I

"BUT SUPPOSE YOUR daughter falls in love with me, sir?" So plainspoken was the inquiry, so clearly couched in real concern, that the young speaker was immediately absolved of any charge of arrogance.

And, indeed, one glance, first at his fine, lithe figure and then at his equally classic countenance, would instantly confirm the validity of his fears for the heart of the lady in question.

The man who strode beside him down the Cornish beach was white-headed and ruddy-faced, of no great height and tending toward portliness, but with an unmistakably military bearing and an air of command. He now turned just such a glance upon his former first lieutenant. His affectionately amused eyes took the measure of the man: the length of leg, the trimness of the waist, the breadth of the shoulders, the cleft in the square jaw, the strong, sweet smile, the aquiline perfection of the nose (a fitting pediment for mesmerizing eyes of a unique gray-blue), the thick, dark locks clipped short in the current fashion, but sufficiently casual in their arrangement to preclude the slightest hint of foppery.

Following this inventory of his junior's attributes, the elder man broke into a gentle chuckle, punctuated by an assured, knowing nod of his head to indicate absolute certainty. Clapping his hand good-naturedly on the elegantly attired back of his companion, he announced rather gaily, "Emma! Fall in love with you! You need have no worries on that score, Lieutenant. My Emma will never develop a *tendre* for you. You're much too silly for her!"

This frank pronouncement hit its mark squarely enough to stop the younger gentleman in his tracks. "*Silly*, Admiral Davenant, sir?"

"Wish I could've used a less brutal word, Marcus, but there ain't any. Point is, you won't enchant my girl in the least. She'll accept you as . . . as . . . hrmph . . . as an expensive gift, but she'll never take you seriously. You're the famous Beau Leicester, and there's nobody Emma has less use for than a beau of the *ton*. My daughter is concerned only with things of the spirit—truth, souls, and the like. She claims to judge a man on the cut of his opinions, not his waistcoat."

"And you, sir." The object of this accusation turned the suddenly solemn gray-blue eyes toward his recent commanding officer and paused an instant to screw up his courage. "And you, Admiral, would you corroborate her opinion? Do you, too, find me silly?"

They were climbing now over the dunes toward a large shelved rock at the base of the low cliffs. As the two men reached this station, Admiral Davenant, breathless from the ascent, slowly seated himself, drew out a lawn handkerchief from his jacket pocket, and mopped his brow before confronting his anxious interlocuter. "Well," he commenced slowly, "I can see in you what she will see. From some aspects, you may appear . . . somewhat . . . silly. But not foolish," he hastened to add. "*Never* foolish. If I'd thought that of you, I wouldn't have summoned you here to help me with Emma."

A faint, dispirited-sounding murmur was the only acknowledgment of this dubious encouragement.

"Marcus, listen to me," Lord Davenant continued, drawing out a flask from his coat and offering it to the shaken young man, who hastily accepted it and brought it to his lips, drinking deeply, as if to staunch the pain of a wound. "My boy," the admiral spoke in the soothing accents of a bearer of bad news, "you are suffering from a handicap that is rare in the world, and rarer still in London." He accepted back the flask, took a healthy swallow himself, and prepared to deliver the dread diagnosis.

"You have committed the unpardonable sin of being born perfect. You are rich, landed, pedigreed, educated, and the handsomest devil in England if not all Europe. You are a capital horseman, a seaman of legend, and a valiant soldier with the courage to walk away from a fool's challenge, or fight to the death if pressed to the point of honor. You are a defender of ladies' virtue, a Corinthian of elegant mien, honorable intent, and exquisite toilette, a sportsman of note and a lucky gambler who can hold his liquor. You are a man's man who is nevertheless adored by animals and children. And of ladies I need not say more. In short, Marcus, you are a fella without faults, and, to an artistic girl such as Emma, a man without faults is a man without qualities. If only you lacked a sense of humor, or took unfair advantage of shopgirls and serving maids, or bit your nails. But even these few peccadilloes are denied you. You are, quite simply, a knight born in the wrong century, especially to a modern girl like my Emma, who considers all soldiers brutes and all gentlemen shallow. She

3

would far rather a troubadour carry her favor than a knight.''

"Troubadour? Any particular troubadour?''

"I'm afraid so.''

"Not Lord Jason!'' Marcus's eyes grew steely with apprehension.

"The very one.''

"Didn't even know he knew your daughter.''

"Alas, all too well. Marcus, put yourself in my place for a moment. Consider your grief upon discovering that the great passion of your only child's life is that infernal scribbler, Jason!'' Lord Davenant fell silent for a moment and stared bleakly out to sea. "Damned rascal. I swear I'd rather she'd have taken up with that wild Byron fella. At least, he affects some semblance of manners. Jason broke my poor girl's heart, ya' know, when he ran off. Almost killed her when she heard he'd taken up with my niece Florissa. Sadder yet, Emma even now waits for him to return.''

"The rogue!'' Marcus seethed with empathetic outrage. "But surely he'd never dare show his face in London, not after the way he bolted.''

"Wouldn't put it past him to come back. He's a man without shame. Never understood what either Emma or Florissa saw in him to begin with. Must say, though, the run-off quite surprised me.'' And he brought the flask once more to his lips before continuing, "Just don't understand these women, Marcus, or what it is they want. Two of 'em, one ruining her health, the other her repute, over a fortune-hunting fop who doesn't know fore from aft. Strange, though, I always fancied—feared is more like it—that Emma would snag him. Still feel she might, actually. Wager he shows up in London any day now. And she *might* just win 'im this go!''

"But, sir,'' Marcus inquired compassionately, "surely you would do your utmost to discourage such an eventuality.''

4

"Might. Might not. Emma's greatly determined. Do her good to have a chance to say no."

"But she'll say yes."

"Oh, no she won't, my boy, not if you're half the teacher I think you are. You're the cleverest chap I know and the bravest, two exemplary traits which are essential in dealing with my daughter. You're going to make an absolutely capital professor of deportment, Marcus, believe me. So go to it! Teach her to flirt, fan, waltz—faint, if you feel it's necessary. First, transform her into a woman any man would crave for a wife. We'll see if Jason retains a place in her heart when honorable men are suing for her hand."

Lord Davenant slapped Marcus on the knee to punctuate his argument. He rose first, well-rested and beaming, and together they made the short descent to the beach in contemplative silence.

Once they had attained the sand, Davenant turned and placed a heavy hand on his former first lieutenant's shoulder, gazing into his eyes: it was as if the commander and his first officer once again shared that sacrosanct moment on the bridge before the first barrage. Davenant's voice rang meaningfully. "Marcus, more than once, in the heat of battle, you have entrusted me with your life." Despite the somber nature of the older man's declaration, Marcus could have sworn he spotted a twinkle in his superior's eyes but it passed before he could be certain. "Now, as on those heroic occasions you vouchsafed to me your very survival, I am vouchsafing to you my daughter."

A new inner torment seemed suddenly to furrow Marcus's brow. He spoke at last. "Sir, there's something you must know about me."

"Nonsense," the admiral countered. "I know quite enough about you already."

"No, sir, you fail to catch my intent. I am promised to a lady . . . or about to be, and—"

"Easy does it, my boy. Just tell her the truth, and prevail upon her to wait some little time. Do your job well, and you'll be in her arms before she even notices you're gone."

"But, sir, I must insist upon explaining myself."

"All right, Marcus, if you must, you must. We'll discuss it later. But for now, say you'll do it, boy. Emma's difficult, but she's a good-hearted lass, and I love her. It grieves me to see her stuck in the doldrums. And since she's alone in the world, without so much as a brother or sister, I've a mind to make certain before I go that both my money and my daughter are well served. Emma's got to find herself a decent husband and soon; and, Marcus, you're the only one who can make her want to and be able to! So, Marcus, I implore you—no, Lieutenant, I order you—before Lord Jason worms his way back into Emma's heart and my holdings, get my daughter wed!"

Chapter II

THE SHINING BLACK barouche had scarcely pulled up before a handsome white house in Belgrave Square when the news of its occupant's arrival had speedily passed from the butler (who had witnessed it from behind the curtain of a front window), to the cook, to the upstairs girl, Lucy; and it was she who, with the extraordinary, innocent valor of the very young, had taken it upon herself to report the forthcoming event to Lady Emma's maid and protectress, Anne Gillings.

To the tender ear of that compassionate soul, the announcement clanged as loudly and painfully as if it had been a curse. And, had you cared to solicit from that gentle lady her more protracted opinion of the imminent visitation, she might well have suggested her preference for a toothache.

As it was, she drew her Amazonian person up to its full,

impressive height, turned a ferret-bright eye on her informant, and coldly inquired, "You are positive?"

"I did not myself see the vehicle, ma'am—" Lucy fearlessly challenged Gillings's burning gaze with a chilly one "—but Harsant assured us he would recognize that black barouche were he lying in his grave."

"So *he's* back—to break her heart a second time, I've no doubt," the protectress snorted, glancing back to assure herself that the door to Lady Emma's bedroom was still firmly shut. "What is to be done, now that he has exhibited the shocking audacity of calling on her? My one hope resides in the good sense she may display by refusing to see him at all."

"But, Miss Gillings, she has been so very sad since he ran off. She is too grieved even to enjoy her books as she used. I think they remind her of him. Perhaps, Miss Gillings, he's come back because he's realized the error of his—"

Lucy's declaration of girlish faith was interrupted by the downstairs bell announcing the controversial subject's presence on their very doorstep. And shortly thereafter, the butler Harsant, his face stony with disapproval, appeared in the sitting room with a card on a silver tray. He spoke as if intoning a eulogy. "Well, Miss Gillings, the worst has come to pass—as, I collect, you already know." He shot a condemning glance at the little maid who had maneuvered to beat him to Miss Gillings with the news.

All three servants sighed in unison and observed a moment of silence, which at length was broken by Miss Gillings. "Harsant, we have no choice but to convey this hateful card to her ladyship and pray she will show the good sense to reject it." And, with that, she seized the tray, walked to the bedroom door, rapped softly, and proceeded into the chamber.

Emma Davenant, twenty-one and tousle-headed beneath a darling cap, sat huddled in the center of a great bed hung with blue silk, her breakfast tray languishing in her lap, her spectacles halfwise down her nose, as she addressed herself to a volume which, pity poor Mr. Keats, was turned upside down without seeming to attract the notice of its reader.

Apparently immersed in the topsy-turvy version of "The Eve of Saint Agnes," she did not acknowledge Miss Gillings's arrival. The poor thing! opined that lady to herself, she is still so deep in despair, so sick with love! And to think that I must be the agent of what can only be fresh anguish. Nonetheless she steeled herself to duty and gently but firmly called out her mistress's name.

Emma, drifting far off in the warm waters of happy memory, abruptly jerked her hand up out of the sea of dreams; it flew in startlement to her breast. "Gillings, you frightened me!"

"Sorry to disturb your reading, ma'am." She glanced pointedly at the book, and Emma, catching her stare in midair and tracing it to its object, ruefully noted the book's alarming condition. Promptly turning it upright, she composed herself and inquired of Gillings, "Has Barnaby returned?"

Gillings was forced to reply in the negative.

"Oh, well," her mistress mused, "I trust he is enjoying himself." Just then she caught sight of the silver tray and demanded sharply, "What are you holding?"

"A card, ma'am."

"Yes, Gillings, but whose?"

"Ma'am . . ."

Deducing the possible identity of the caller from Gillings's uncharacteristic hesitancy, Emma allowed herself to hope against hope as a sweet stab of exhilaration pierced her. "Who is here, Gillings?" she demanded, more tremulously.

9

Turning the hue of a fresh-boiled lobster, Gillings wordlessly proferred the tray to her impatient mistress who proceeded at once to snatch the card from its silver resting place. She pushed up her spectacles, swiftly perused it, and blanched—her extreme pallor an ivory complement to Gillings's crimson color.

"Simon! Here?" gasped Emma, grown so vaporish with the news that she dropped her book, which fell onto the breakfast tray, spewing muffins and upsetting a small pitcher of cream, which liquid dared to course off the tray, flow onto the coverlet, and run in rivulets over milady's night-gown, quite soaking it without so much as capturing her attention.

"Lord Jason awaits you in the burgundy saloon, ma'am." It was only by exercising the most Herculean effort of restraint that Gillings banished from her lips the fearful warning her warm heart would rehearse to that announcement. And it was only through an even greater agony of self-containment that she demurred to solicit her mistress's response before that pale lady was prepared to deliver it.

So it was that several minutes passed before Emma broke the trance that the wicked card had cast upon her by raising her eyes, collecting herself, and speaking firmly in a voice that trembled almost imperceptibly. "Gillings, since I am obviously indisposed and in no condition to receive callers, please proceed to the burgundy saloon and extend to Lord Jason my sincerest regrets." At the conclusion of these instructions, Emma once more took up her book (into which, it must be admitted, she slipped the dismissed card) and resumed her perusal of Mr. Keats's work. That the volume was once more turned roundabout was thought by a relieved Miss Gillings not worth mentioning. Still the servant could not resist a smallish smile as she moved proudly toward the door. "Yes, milady," she purred. "I'll go at once." Relief having speeded her step, the good lady had reached the doorway and was almost through it before the word she had dreaded to hear struck her with a rapier sting. "Wait!"

The smile instantly fled from Gillings's mouth to be replaced by a most definite frown as she wheeled reluctantly about and muttered, "I beg your pardon, madame."

"Wait! Don't go! Annie! Oh, Annie! He's come back! All the way from Venice. How can I not receive him? Does he look sad?"

Gillings's only response was a sniff of dismissal, not sufficiently pointed to prevent her ladyship from suddenly shooting up and pushing away the tray onto which the volume had once again fallen to leap from the bed, mindless of her dripping nightgown or the muffins under her feet.

"Oh, I must see him. It would be too rude! What shall I wear? I can never remember whether or not it is the thing to wear muslin at this time of day . . . Annie, what if he doesn't wait? He may have other appointments! But I can't go downstairs like this! And my hair's hopeless! Annie, dear Annie."

Although her treasured charge had run to her, seizing her hand in supplication, Miss Gillings remained coldly impervious. Still Emma persisted, "Please, *please* go downstairs and be sure you detain him! Then rush back up with Lucy to help with my toilette. Will you do it now, Annie? He may be preparing to depart even as we speak. Will you go to him?"

Despite her conviction that her collaboration would constitute a mortal sin against her darling girl, Gillings felt her resolve fleeing. And it had to be admitted that the merest mention of Lord Jason's name had brought the long-dimmed

sparkle back into Emma's eyes again. "Very well, miss."
Slowly and solemnly she again marched to the door, this
time accompanied by the peal of breathless "hurries"
issuing from the already open wardrobe.

Chapter III

LADY EMMA DAVENANT, late of the Cornish cliffs, presently of 10 Belgrave Square, London, squinted contemplatively at her sadly blurred reflection in the gilt-edged standing mirror, then proceeded to wrinkle her nose. Although the forfeiture of her spectacles made any opinion of her just-completed toilette less than definitive, she had to admit to a lack of perfect satisfaction.

Granted, the maize-hued muslin frock, embroidered with a thousand tiny cornflowers, was greatly complemented by the sky blue of her China silk overdress; granted, the troublesome auburn curls—under Gillings's militant supervision—had been whipped into submission by a cleverly camouflaged batallion of hairpins and golden blossoms; granted, the contribution of a touch of rouge on her cheeks and lips had helped to restore some color to her ashen countenance. Still—did not the yellow turn her sallow? And did not the delicacy of her costume only serve to emphasize what even those who loved her were forced to acknowledge as awkwardness? Could she, further, navigate the descent to the burgundy saloon without tripping in the sandals? And, if she tripped, would not her hair seize the chance to escape its restraints and plunge in rowdy freedom to her shoulders? And who could deny her lips were too full and her cheekbones too pronounced for rouge? And even the most lovesick swain must find it difficult not to adjudge her hair too red, her eyes too green, her gown too blue, her person entirely too loudly colorful to receive anyone in a burgundy saloon?

Worst of all, she felt certain, were the very green eyes which Simon had once praised in a birthday ode as "orbs limpid with the distant cast of gentle dreams," but which, if the truth be told, were near-sighted. Though Lord Jason might find her soft, unsteady gaze to his poetic liking, she, without the hateful spectacles, was quite unable to see her own reflection sharply enough even to be able to second his opinion.

Nor could Society. Too early in her London trials, Emma had been forced—and painfully—to the understanding that good *ton* and bad eyesight would never make a match.

Oh, she had sadly learned more lessons than that since her London arrival. She had learned, for instance, that the only fate worse for a lady of fashion than the wearing of spectacles was the display of a country-bred innocence that passed too easily for ignorance. And to be not only a bumpkin but a half-blind one at that was—in the graceful world of Almack's and the Vauxhall—worse than bearing the awful countenance of the undeniably ugly but enormously sophisticated and clear-sighted likes of Lady Slightword or the Duchess of Blore.

Raised in the rockbound wilds of Cornwall by an eminent but often absent widowed father, Emma had passed a sheltered girlhood consuming novels of London high life as if they had been so many tea cakes. And, indeed, her appetite for the *ton* had only been whetted by these wonderfully addicting confections in which snoozed the grand design of her destiny. For what triumphs could London not pledge a young female of vivacity, pedigree, and a not insubstantial fortune?

After all, she was no simple cleric's daughter in hand-me-down homespun, dreaming by the side of a peat fire in a decrepit and overpopulated Yorkshire parsonage. No, *she* was Lady Emma Davenant, only child and heir to Admiral Sir William Davenant, Duke of Penzance, First Sea Lord (ret.), whose holdings extended considerably beyond Cornwall to include a large estate in Donegal and the most picturesque of Tudor villages in Devon, not to mention the spanking new town house in that latest souvenir of Bavesi and Cubitt's architectural acumen, Belgrave Square.

Here, impelled by Emma's demure but relentless passion to live out her childhood dreams, the admiral had agreed to install his daughter in properly high fashion. Likewise, at Emma's urging, he had agreed to procure a Society tutor, wise in the ways of the world, who would instruct the fledgling belle in all the requisites: what to say to the Austrian ambassador over the fish course; how to flirt with a Pink of the *ton* without betraying a hint of nervousness or desperation; which redingote went best in Rotten Row, what reticule at a route party. In short, to inculcate in Emma's already whirling head the concise grammar of husband stalking, whose rules were as inflexible as those that governed Latin conjugations and which were intended to become as second to her nature as *amo, amas, amat*.

But whom to choose? There were always the aging emigrée beauties whose firsthand accounts of last-minute escapes from the guillotine were grown as faded as their faces and as interminable as their chatter. No French woman. Especially not now that *à la française* was *toute passée* in the fairy tale halls of Carleton House.

Still available was the personal maid of Lady Caroline Lamb, now that the scandalous toast of the *ton* had committed the multiple crime of having (first) fled her marriage bed to (second) run off to (third) the Continent to (fourth) live openly with (fifth) a writer. But Lady Caroline's maid would long languish at liberty, since her notorious influence over her mistress's unusual behavior was thought to make her more unwelcome than the pox in any decent lady's chambers.

Several venerable *grandes dames* were known to sponsor young gentlewomen's come-outs, but they were too stuffy or too tired of it all or too concerned with launching their daughters' daughters seriously to take on an outside protégée. And the granddaughters themselves (encouraged by these very grandmothers) were much too hot in pursuit of the *rara avis* ever to welcome a new Diana to the husband hunt. Fops could be bought, of course, but, without exception, they were too entranced with themselves to concentrate on any style but their own.

Hélas! But just when all ideas had been dismissed and all avenues exhausted, when Emma had only the air on which to put her foot down, the letter came.

That mauve paper, that blue crest, that Vienna frank, those delicate sheets scented with a fragrance soon to become fatally familiar—it was all so smart, so very pretty, so *haut monde*, that even unread, it produced in Emma a heady admixture of exhilaration and foreboding. Holding the graceful note before her, she knew that it would never—and could never—have come so from her, and that disturbed her. But, after studying the sleek and stylish epistle, her yearning for London glamour once again reclaimed her

16

soul, and she knew as well that someday soon her own stationery would put the mauve paper to shame. Besides, Emma's penmanship was better, more refined than the illegible chick-scratch which resisted deciphering.

But once that self-same farrago was unpuzzled, it was found to contain an offering which would speedily deliver Emma out of her present dilemma: Lady Florissa de Coucy, daughter to the Duke of Penzance's late sister-in-law, having heard (even in Vienna, where she was visiting friends) of Emma's arrival in London, was, out of affectionate regard for the happy times she and her cousin had shared as children, delighted to proffer that same dear little cousin her tireless support in aid of the perfect London come-out.

For an instant the child Florissa flashed across Emma's memory as pure astronomy: a trailing comet—too hot, too blindingly light, too mercurial, even at seven, to seek out the company of an infinitely slower, dear little star from Cornwall. But times change, rivalries diminish, and what was first recollected as a girlish contest for grown-up attention came to be transmuted into the merriest of *nostalgies*.

Memories being more elusive even than social tutors, the invitation was accepted, and the date of arrival fixed. And so it was that Florissa de Coucy came dancing into 10 Belgrave Square.

Not that she literally danced, but to a horrified Emma, she seemed to: her lush ebony locks streaked a glowing silver by the rays of sunlight which always seemed to be streaming in the window behind her; her deep blue eyes skipping lightly from face to face, allowing the limitless lashes to dip down toward alabaster cheeks when so much admiration provoked a moment of modesty; those cherry-red lips, inexplicably moist; the crystalline peals of laughter; the wasp waist and delicate lobes. Here was *ton*—all elegance and irresistible femininity. Here, unbearably, was the confirmation of that foreboding Emma had felt while holding the letter, for, standing before her was the woman she had always dreamed of becoming and now knew she could never be.

Of course, Florissa took command of the staff at once, and Emma, having gotten precisely what she had so carefully asked for, brooded each day and night until sleep claimed her, the bitter tears of Pyrrhic victory soaking the damask beneath her cheek.

Jealousy is a poor student, and competition often forces the challenger, fatally, to see only the rival's frailties. Unable to bear Florissa's seemingly effortless ascension to the position of mistress of the house, Emma felt her nature turning down, and she spent long hours sulking over the bloodless coup which had thrust her from the throne.

It was so unfair, so undeserved! The staff, to a person, was clearly wanton, fickle and easily deceived, for, surely, only by the foulest of deceptions could these good folks allow themselves to drift blissfully away from her own gentle moorings.

And, if it were deception, who could the deceiver be but the hideous Florissa herself? Suddenly the cousin's entire performance revealed itself to Emma as an intricate sequence of falsities: Florissa's generosity masked expediency; her warmth was greed; her dazzling disposition merely a disguise for a cold, manipulative heart. She was ill-read and indicated no interest in learning anything but the newest dance. She was too loud when she laughed and much too forward. Too shallow to know the meaning of love, Florissa was interested only in pursuit and conquest. And her feet were large.

Looking back, Emma saw her own error. It was not that her judgment of her fabulous cousin was entirely wrong—in fact, subsequent events had proven her to be not altogether off target in her cataloging of Florissa's ethical flaws. It was not that she had perceived her incorrectly; rather, that she had not perceived her completely, had missed appreciating the rules of charm, which Florissa had mastered to perfection and which, in a less tempestuous setting, Emma could have calmly observed and refined to her own taste. Instead, the fallen star retreated into the fancy that emulation is flattery, and that, even if she had to tiptoe through London in Florissa's shadow, she would never imitate her! And so it was that Emma matched Florissa's crystalline conversation with sullen silences; her warmth with iciness; her grace with stiffness.

At Almack's, as every beau of note pressed Florissa for dance after dance, Emma, feeling mildewed in wet muslin, discouraged any promising partner's invitation before he could ask by turning on him a glance that withered the world. When shopping in Bond Street or Jermyn Street, Florissa and Emma were frequently stopped by gentlemen of the former's acquaintance who urged her (and her cousin . . . Emma, was it?) to accompany them to St. James's Park for a turnabout in the sunlight. Florissa would eagerly accept, but Emma would decline, claiming a megrim, and the promise of a merry outing would fall by the wayside.

Watching Florissa chat and flirt and ensorcel her partners at dinner only served to make Emma more aware that she had no small talk. She sat in silence, therefore, ignored finally by neighbors she so utterly dismissed that they rarely remembered her . . . except as Florissa's cousin.

So this was London! This was *ton*—the world Emma had dreamed of conquering overnight. Alas for her dreams for it had all turned devilishly against her.

Until she met Simon. Simon, dark and magnificently moody, brilliant as a shooting star, silent as she. Simon, who talked only with her, sought her out, called upon her. Simon, whom she had loved at first sight and continued to love, though the shock of his run-off and his subsequent Venetian liaison with Florissa had sent her to her bed, half-crazed with grief and jealousy.

Yes, her beloved Simon had left her; but now, miraculously, he had returned to London, to Belgrave Square, to the burgundy saloon, where his presence positively proved to Emma that she had been more charming than Florissa all along.

Chapter IV

EMMA, HAVING NEGOTIATED the threatening course of the grand staircase (by clinging to the railing with both hands and proceeding step by step with a precision worthy of a military tattoo), took courage, tripping only once and that slightly, and began a slow march across the hall to the door of the burgundy saloon.

Halfwise across the hall, she was halted in her progress by the plump yet dignified form of Harsant the butler, who loomed out of nowhere; urgency was quietly conveyed beneath the absolute calm of his demeanor.

"Madame," he offered.

"Not now, Harsant," snapped his mistress, anxious to recapture her heart, which awaited her in the burgundy saloon.

"But, madame," the butler persevered.

"I said later, Harsant," she reiterated, punctuating the

command with a long stride that provoked a listing of her carriage. Those sandals!

"As you like, madame." Only the most astute of observers would have apprehended the sigh contained within the clipped response, as he led Emma to the door and opened it before her.

Did her heart actually stop in that instant when the door fell back? Or would it happen as she crossed the threshold? Then, surely, her delicate motor, fatally overwhelmed, would propel her to the floor, dead as a doornail. Well, if it were death that would greet her in the burgundy saloon, she, an admiral's daughter, would meet it face on without so much as a tremble. Too late now to rehearse the first words, to choose the posture, to assume the regard she desired to present to him. Too late to set the scene, as Florissa would have done, too late—

He was sitting with his back to her, facing the fireplace in an armchair of burgundy brocade and gilded wood, hunched over as if in meditation. And that first sight did, indeed, stun her, for the comforting familiarity of his form had vanished. His whole body seemed to have altered, his bearing changed. He was a stranger! He had gone away the Simon she loved and returned a man she scarcely recognized.

And then he turned. And rose. And she knew with certainty that the shock of his visit had driven her quite mad. For standing before her was the handsomest man she had ever seen or dreamed of seeing. A vision. But not of Simon.

"You're not Simon!"

"No, actually, I'm not." The stranger offered no more.

"But he was here! What's happened to him?"

"As he explained it, he'd been waiting for some time. And since he was to meet a friend at Watier's five minutes hence, he ran off, leaving me to advise you he will return as soon as he can discharge the obligation. He asked me to express his apologies for the inconvenience, but said it could not be helped.''

I knew it, Emma chastised herself, I knew it! The shock of anticlimax had so overwhelmed her that only by the sheerest force of her will could she contain the tears which unexpectedly threatened to spring forth. For an instant her vision of the room, of the world, shrank to a single point of light—a pinprick containing the clear but strangely disturbing image of a man so handsome that his beauty was palpable even to the unspectacled.

''And who, may I ask, are you?'' Emma demanded in a tone, balmy as an Arctic morn.

''I'm Marcus Leicester,'' he allowed, persisting in his accursedly pleasant manner despite her chilliness.

''Marcus Leicester, *the* Marcus Leicester? You are?'' The fury of her recent disappointment had held her fast to a spot in dead center of the room, her arms rigid as sticks at her sides, her fingers balled into fists of frustration. But now that the famous name was uttered, she was stunned out of her angry posture by a dizzying wave of fresh astonishment.

''Sorry to be the cause of your discomfiture, Lady Emma.'' And with that, the Adonis rose to his full Augustan height and walked gracefully toward her. Before she could either shrink back or wither him with a forbidding look, he had grasped her hand and drawn it gently to his lips.

Surely her long days of mourning Simon had addled her brain! Certainly her present disappointment had propelled her beyond the pale! Clearly had she her wits about her, she would recognize that this was a mirage which stood before her, its warm and generous imaginary lips pressed to her hand. Surely, after all, he was a vision. But not just any vision! Rather a vision of the most legendary Corinthian of them all, the Beau Leicester! In Emma Davenant's burgundy saloon! How extraordinary!

Emma was forced to quiet her musings by the sudden awareness not only that the vision still retained her hand, but had also trained his amazingly pellucid sea-gray eyes upon her more mundane green ones. Wake up, Emma!

"Lord Leicester," her voice emerged a shade warmer than she had intended. "What brings you to Belgrave Square?" Disengaging her hand, she swept to a small silk love seat, arranged herself, then motioned him to take a chair opposite.

"I am sent by your father."

The shocking response took Emma up in the air, spun her about, and landed her in a whirlpool of dangerous suspicions. "By my father? As what?"

Exquisitely settling himself into his chair which should have been several sizes too small for him, he met her gaze and announced, "As a birthday gift, milady."

"As a birthday gift?" she pursued in a clearly dubious tone. (First, her birthday was still three months away, in June. Secondly, even in the jaded world of Society, the presentation of beaux to inexperienced young women as keepsakes was too bizarre a style to have originated with one's father.)

"May I smoke?" He had extracted from the inner pocket of his faultlessly fitted green gabardine coat a slender brown cylinder the length of a man's finger, and a match which, following her consent, he proceeded to strike on the bottom of his smart mahogany boots. He placed the odd brown object between his lovely lips. Then he brought the flame to the slim cylinder and inhaled deeply. When he languidly expelled the smoke, it was in absolutely perfect rings. Glancing casually at the little tube now smoking aromatically between his fingers, he commented, "Nasty habit, I admit. Plan to stop it altogether. Picked it up in St.

24

Croix when I traveled there. Can't find 'em in this part of the world. Have to have them ordered specially from the planters, who smoke 'em there. Called *cigarettes*." He cavalierly flicked the ash which had formed on the cigarette into the fireplace. "Now, about my purpose here . . ."

"Yes?" Emma hoped he'd caught the note of unyielding skepticism in her tone.

"Well, now," he continued, seeming to grow—could it be?—almost sheepish. "I had the great honor to serve under your father in the Peninsula where I was his first officer. Following the happy conclusion of that encounter, I set off to see what the world had to offer, traveling to St. Petersburg, to Vienna and Amsterdam, to Italy and Greece, and on to the far-flung cities of America: New York, Philadelphia, and Boston, thence south to New Orleans and farther to the Floridas and beyond. After a sojourn abroad of some two years' duration, I arrived back in London and went directly to my lodgings in Cheyne Walk . . . Do you know Cheyne Walk?"

"I am not sure."

"It's a beautiful little street on the Embankment at Chelsea. Quite old. The very place to stroll along the river with a partner."

"Yes? I'll remember that," commented Emma with more than a hint of archness.

"To continue. I returned to Cheyne Walk to find awaiting me a message from your father, bidding me to Cornwall on a matter of great urgency."

"So you went."

"Of course."

"And . . ."

"And when I arrived, your father—" he paused here, taking a rather deep breath. "Lady Emma, I feel I must be blunt with you." Although his manner had grown no less intent, Emma was positive she could sense in him some incipient—heaven forfend!—embarrassment. What had Father taken it into his head to do?

"Your father inquired into the state of my finances, having heard that my holdings had sustained grave setbacks during my long absence. I was forced to confess that I found myself penniless."

"Oh Lord, he's bought him!" she gasped inwardly.

Reading her thoughts, the gentleman hastened to assuage her concern. "But let me assure you, Lady Emma, your father did *not* buy me." Her relief was sudden ecstasy.

"He rented me."

"Rented you?"

"Well, yes. Your father allowed as to how you'd been searching for someone to drill you in *ton*; and since I am schooled in the observation and practice of Society, Admiral Davenant engaged me to instruct you."

"You must have been very expensive," Emma murmured through her renewed astonishment.

"Yes, very." The earnestness of his reply struck her unpleasantly. Was he humorless, as well as rented?

"How kind and how . . . unconventional . . . of my father! Unfortunately he failed to inform you that I shall be returning to Cornwall almost at once."

"Returning to Cornwall?"

"Yes. I have been in London for nearly six months and find I tire of it." *Toute soignée*, she sat back in her seat, languidly brushing an invisible curl from her forehead with a delicate hand. "So you see, I won't be needing your services."

"Leaving London, Lady Emma? Even now that Lord Jason has returned?"

"And what possible difference should that make?"

"Frankly, ma'am, Lord Jason's *tendre* for you was the talk of the Continent. There are those who say he left Florissa de Coucy's arms for yours." Marcus, who, in the

26

service of his own character, made it a point always to tell the truth, found himself aghast at how smoothly the lies slid from his lips.

"So you could teach me how to make Lord Jason declare himself?"

"Certainly, Lady Emma, if such is your desire. After all, I am your servant."

Emma, still staring into the sympathetic depths of those gray-blue pools, could barely stifle a giggle of excitement. "Yes, you *are* my servant, and Lord Jason *is* my desire. Hm. Were I to accept you, how would our lessons proceed?"

The prospective love teacher, having smoked his cigarette down almost to his fingertips, seemed to notice the stub for the first time and hurled it with spirit into the fire. "First, we'll have private instruction—what to wear, how to speak, how to dance, et al. Then we'll go on to public instruction. As your escort, I'll walk you through every sort of social occasion—dinner parties, routes, masquerades, teas—and show you Almack's, the Vauxhall Gardens, the Serpentine, even Carleton House. Your education will culminate in your great birthday ball, three months hence."

"And the nature of our association shall . . . remain . . . between us?"

"Most assuredly. So far as the *ton* is concerned, I shall have arrived back in London, met you, and developed a *tendre* for you—and, perhaps, for your fortune, as well. Frankly it is good to be seen on my arm, and it may encourage Lord Jason to a frenzy of jealousy in which he loses control and declares himself."

One was forced to consider the possibility that the gods had sent this unlikely cupid to one's burgundy saloon. Just as one had to admit that the cupid's proposal was, undeniably, of more than passing interest. Nevertheless some slight doubt persisted. "But Lord Jason has always been so uncommitted," she rather too kindly remarked.

"Ah, Lady Emma, only in your presence. He is known to be . . . intimidated by you. After all, you are no silly belle of the *ton*. You are a woman of great imagination and strong convictions, who demands the same high standards of behavior from others as you do from yourself." Was she riveted more by the words or the gray-blue eyes? "You strive, Lady Emma, for an independence of mien and a clarity of purpose more common to the battlefield than the ballroom." She found his words striking an inner chord that was all too responsive for comfort. "To draw out a man's true intention, you must not challenge him; rather, you must sweeten him, soften his resolve, put his sense of argument to sleep. You must—like a *saboteur*— come in the night, catch the quarry off guard, and disarm and overwhelm him. You must learn that, in affairs of the heart, pretense may be the most appropriate conveyance of honesty."

"Are you suggesting that I corrupt a friendship founded on purity of purpose?"

"Yes, Lady Emma, that is precisely what I suggest. After all, ma'am, does one graciously invite a deer to confront the hunter? Do we expect a quail to arise from the bush to announce his presence to the archer? No, love is strategy, and strategy is stealthy, and since I am a beau as well as a soldier, I am consummately practiced in both arenas. Granted, I have need of the money; but you have need of Lord Jason. I suggest that this arrangement can be of mutual advantage."

Emma allowed her guard to slip a bit further. "You could really show me how to captivate Lord Jason?"

He nodded confidently, his eyes still on hers.

"Well, Lord Leicester—"

Emma had only just commenced when the door burst open, the voice she had so longed to hear shouted, "Emma!" and Lord Jason bounded into the room.

As her spirit shifted like a kaleidoscope to a dazzling new pattern of delight, Emma thought to swoon. Yet, in the instant it took Simon to reach her side and drop to his knees, she recovered herself sufficiently to require for steadiness only one hand poised lightly on her chair. The other was free for him to capture and secure with a kiss. Only then did he allow his ardent eyes to greet her unbelieving ones.

And as he gazed at her, all tender seriousness, Emma was struck again by what she had always seen as the beguiling sweetness of his ice-blue eyes, by what she knew to be his youthful shyness, though others might call it sullenness. His solemn smile was as charming to her as ever, his very presence an absolute delight.

And as the pain of recent loss retreated before the joy of rediscovery, Emma regally lifted her head and bade him rise.

Taking both her hands in his, Simon now proclaimed, "Emma! Emma!" His tone was every bit as passionate as she'd hoped, almost pained in its ardor. And the anguish he offered up to her as the currency of his atonement touched her heart. "Emma," he murmured again, "Emma, my dear, I'm home!"

Suddenly, inexplicably, she was reminded of the third party in the saloon, and momentarily forsook her lover to search out her beau. He was nowhere to be seen, making her wonder if perhaps she *had* imagined him after all. But soon her fears were laid to rest. Simon had evidently seen (and ignored) him, for now he commented dryly, "Decent of Leicester to sneak off quietly—" the pause was punctuated with a sharp little grin "—once he realized he was . . . intruding." And again he grasped her hands, all smiles. "Emma, how good to see you, dear friend!"

Friend! At once the cloud of happiness upon which she

had momentarily floated quite dissolved, and she tumbled back to earth. Friend! That hated word! After what she'd suffered!

Her disappointment must have cast a shadow across her countenance, for Simon stepped back, furrowed his brow in an expression of great concern, and inquired, "But, Emma, whatever is wrong? You seem to be in sudden discomfort."

"Oh, no!" she hastened to reply. "I'm quite fine, really. Just a twinge of megrim."

"Megrim? Have you been less than well?"

She could only respond with that labored levity which attempts to spare a loved one a hard truth. "No, not ill precisely . . ."

"Aha!" he nodded in complete understanding. "I know too well the slings and arrows that flesh is heir to. On the passage back, I had the devil of an *ague*. Sneezed and coughed for days. Nose all stuffed up. There were moments when I could tell the ship's doctor was afraid he'd lose me. He played brave in front of me, of course, but I could see right through his cavalier manner. Miraculously, one day, the crisis passed, and I am here to prove it!"

"You seem quite recovered," Emma heard herself calmly say, "except, perhaps, for that slight redness about the nose."

"Oh!" His hand flew to that roseate appurtenance. "Is it so noticeable?"

"Of course not," she assured him, suppressing her vague annoyance at the fact that the conversation had shifted so rapidly from her health to his vanity.

"You are positive it is not disfiguring?" His earnest gaze implored her most frank appraisal.

"Absolutely," she smiled wanly.

"I am so glad," and he once again grasped her hand and kissed it, overcome, apparently, by his gratitude to her for finding his nose perfectly fit. This kiss, luckily, was less protracted than the last, and soon he had once again dropped her hand and stepped back to study her.

"You are looking capital, Emma!"

"As are you, Simon."

"Ah, you have noticed my new Italian cape, I expect. Quite the thing in Venice, you know. No beau worth his gambling debts would even consider being seen in a great-coat this season. I think the black is most dramatic, especially for a fellow in my line of work."

"Yes," she replied. "It enhances the poetic character of your presence."

"And," he beamed, "since we speak of poetry, I have brought you a gift!"

Two gifts in fewer hours, Emma noted. But this one won't have blue-gray eyes.

Simon reached into the breast pocket of his coat and extracted a slim, morocco-leather-bound volume. Sinking once more upon his knee, he slowly extended the book toward the lady, both arms outstretched and his palms meeting to form the salver for the Grail. "To Emma," he intoned. The solemnity of his voice mellowed to a coo as he added, "the first copy!"

She took the volume from his hands into her own; in her spectacleless state, she was forced to raise it perilously close to her nose before deciphering the stamped gold letter as *The Idylls of Sir Percival: A Lay of Courtly Love.*

"Simon!" she exclaimed. "Your poem!"

"*Our* poem, dear Emma," he responded in generous tones. "Yours and mine."

And, indeed, she could hardly have banished from her memory those many, many hours during which they had met over his poetry. Theirs were two minds so perfectly tuned that his *mot juste* was always on the tip of her tongue.

31

Yes, *Idylls* was rightly theirs, a symbol of their precious bond.

"Fresh from the printer's, Emma," Simon continued with considerable animation. "Available only just this morning! Publisher's got great hopes for our little book. You know . . ." An idea seemed to strike him of a sudden. "I say, Emma," he explained as he bolted up from his knees. "I haven't been back so much as a day, but I yearn to take a turn around London. Maybe try the Serpentine to see who's in town."

She smiled in assent, and turned to place the treasured volume on an inlaid chinoiserie table. But, before it could find its resting place, it was snatched from her hand by Simon, who replaced the volume in his pocket. "You are the first person, besides me, to see it," he said warmly as if to clarify that that great privilege *was* his promised gift to her.

Did it occur to her, then, that in his absence she had come to think of him without flaws? That the Simon of her dreams possessed a perfect nobility to which Simon's Simon might never aspire? Or was it rather, that with the image of compassionate eyes and a gentle manner still clear in her mind, Simon's presence seemed subtly altered, suffering the inevitable comparison?

But these disturbing thoughts did not long persevere for the sting of reality faded quickly in the face of her apparent larger triumph. Simon had returned for her! And he wanted Society to know it! Stopping only to collect her bonnet, the couple ran merrily out of the house and on to the Serpentine.

Pausing on the topmost step of 10 Belgrave Square, Marcus Leicester had breathed deeply the uniquely piquant air of a London April and determined to stroll back to Chelsea.

Descending the front steps, he had dismissed his coachman, who waited at the curb in a vintage curricle that was no match for the black barouche parked before it. As he crossed the square and headed toward the river, Marcus found himself prevented from fully imbibing the exotic liquor of English spring by the weight of his thoughts on the mission ahead.

London danced in a carnival of expansion. From Belgravia east, sinuous white houses, arranged in long crescent rows, elegant as beautiful women and just as graceful, proclaimed the energy of the time and the genius of Nash, Bavesi, and Cubitt. Such simplicity—and, yet, such intricacy! But Marcus knew that, compared to the circles within circles into which his assignment would take him, round houses were simple as thatched cottages. Still . . .

Lord Davenant had painted rather too bleak a picture of his troublesome daughter. In fact, Marcus now questioned whether the roots of Emma's difficulties did not in fact derive from her father's overly harsh judgment of her.

Granted, she was less than entirely at ease in company, and her anxiety aggravated the sharpness of her character, as well as her oddly uncoordinated deportment, either of which was sufficient to send any man off to the next woman in prospect. But, beneath all that, Marcus could sense her terror, her shyness and modesty, and her warmth, even passion: her innocent grief for dreams dead—or delayed.

She was, certainly, bright, and, possibly, mischievous, and these qualities were *comme il faut* in the flirting game. Her gaze was a trifle foggy, but it might, with practice, come to be interpreted as seductive. Her temper promised hurricanes, but spirit, when properly managed, was a good thing in a girl.

And she was pretty. Not the siren brunette of a Florissa de Coucy. Nor the boyish-womanish blond of a Caroline

Lamb. No, Emma was . . . he searched for the word . . . Emma could be . . . *adorable*. But whoever had dressed her in that blue and yellow nightmare, which, against a burgundy background, could bring on the vapours in a strong man? And who had applied the rouge with a trowel? Why did she walk as if her feet were bound, grabbing one piece of furniture after another, moving across the room in stages, as if she were for the first time skating across a frozen lake? And why was her hair arranged in a style so clearly antagonistic to its natural inclination?

Oh, there was work to be done, all right; but, surely, it wasn't hopeless. She had the stuff to pull it off, he was certain of that now. And, if she would only allow him to tutor her, there was no reason a decent fellow might not present himself and take her away from that wretch, Jason.

That wresting of Emma's allegiance from the poet was Marcus's paramount concern, and he was fully conscious that it would present no inconsiderable problem. He had, of course, briefly witnessed the couple's reunion in the burgundy saloon. He had seen the short, slight figure, dusty blond curls clustering over the brooding brow, ice-blue eyes mesmerizing Emma in a single glance. And the dramatic black cape thrown back over a black coat, worn over a voluminous shirt with a peculiarly extravagant collar, black pantaloons, and brilliant black boots. Ah, yes! the very apotheosis of the *artiste*.

Jason had run to Emma, thrown himself at her feet, ignoring Marcus's presence entirely, and kissed her hand with considerable passion. She, in response, had placed her other hand on the aureole of his curls just lightly enough to convey her unalloyed adoration.

All too aware that the scene he witnessed was rather too *intime* to sustain a third party, Marcus had taken his hasty leave, suggesting to an unhearing, unresponsive Emma that he would call upon her the following day. Then,

34

hurrying out, he had tripped over a huge gray cat which had silently stationed itself by the door, apparently for the purpose of watching the scene unfolding within. As Marcus careened over the animal to find himself on his knees in the doorway, he looked back at the couple, who were too intent on each other to take note of his plight. Only the great gray cat, unruffled by the collision, deigned to toss him an answering glance which, to Marcus's eye, seemed to contain the merest hint of a smirk. But cats do not smirk—any more than pinks of the *ton* trip over them— and Marcus decided to attribute this momentary loss of equilibrium to random chance, nothing more.

Now, pulling himself out of his reverie, Marcus found himself in the King's Road, so called because it had been built by Charles II as a private route by which he could be conveyed from his palace directly to his mistress's dwelling. Alas, poor Nell Gwyn's house was become a hospital, and any brute who fancied could ride down Charlie's highway. The things men do for women! And the roads down which they are lured in the name of love!

For Emma's benefit, he had compared love to military strategy; but, really, he had the suspicion that love was much less fairly fought than war. Why, the very story he had told her about their situation had been filled with falsities and omissions!

"Marcus, my boy," Admiral Davenant had cautioned him, "be sure she thinks I've bought you off. If she believes I'm presuming on you, she'll have no part of the scheme. And Marcus," he added musingly, "about the other matter: you needn't mention it at all. And she'll never find out otherwise, if we're reasonably careful."

Marcus had questioned the sagacity of that decision, but finally had deferred to the will of his commanding officer.

As a consequence he had by now acquired too many

private lives to sleep sound nights. So he hurried back to Cheyne Walk to set down the letter he had been composing in his head for days and to enjoy a little solitude before the battle commenced.

Chapter V

NOT LONG AFTER Marcus had ventured forth to Chelsea
on foot, two other familiar figures were flying in a black
barouche toward that haughtiest of watery bodies, the
Serpentine. The great cyclorama of Hyde Park presented
itself to their delighted regard as the sparkling water,
smooth as a swan's trail, grasped the sun's rays for an
instant before hurling them forth in blinding bursts of
light. Around them, the *ton*, in a setting magnificently
arranged to flatter itself, from sylvan glades to swan lakes.
Every beau and his latest *tendre* must walk here as an
announcement to Society of the seriousness of mutual
intentions; former enemies casually strolled together in
public acknowledgment that the lady in the case was quite
forgotten. Here were *grandes dames* with their blossoming
granddaughters; elegant young mothers and naughty children and their nurses; lap dogs, whippets, and an occasional collie; the fops, in peacock pairs; and the rakes,
in single-minded pursuit of female quarry.

The rarefied ambiance of the Serpentine had always reminded Emma of her father's orchid garden in Cornwall—the perfume too sweet, the colors too lush, the glamour almost stifling. This was a dizzyingly sensual landscape in which exquisiteness ran riot, with each perfectly beautiful creature showing itself more perfect than the rest of the dazzling crowd.

Emma had always feared the Serpentine, with the twin but conflicting terrors of the shy: being laughed at and being ignored. Today, however, with the man she loved by her side and a private cupid in her back pocket, she was ready to brave Society. Still, as Simon handed her down from the barouche, she instinctively tensed, as if to ward off any unforeseen blows to her newly regained poise. And surely this *tableau vivant* of fashion and frivolity was sufficient to shrivel the confidence of many far more practiced than she.

Simon, on the other hand, displayed no such reticence. On the contrary, he had scarcely escorted her across the grass to an excellent site by the lake, when a particular figure caught his eye, causing him to shout, "Chase! Anthony Chase!" and thence to make straight for the fellow, with Emma following in his wake.

Anthony Chase was, in the near-sighted view, a voguish man of about thirty. His oversized head, which displayed a face full of gigantic features, sat heavily upon a stocky frame. He was dressed parrot fashion in a coat of jade green over fawn pantaloons, accompanied by a green, pink, and yellow-striped waistcoat over a maize shirt, and a surprisingly snowy cravat arranged in the most elaborate fashion. His unfortunately sparse curls were arranged to sweep across his substantial dome, which still shone through like the sun behind bare trees in winter. From head to foot, he sparkled like the Serpentine itself, and the quizzing glass he now lifted to his left eye reflected the shining scene before him. Emma had met Sir Anthony many times in company, but he never seemed to recollect her on their next meeting, and this encounter promised more of the same, for he turned directly to her companion.

"I say, Jason. Nice to have you . . . back," he murmured. Was his barely perceptible hesitation meant to convey that Jason had not yet been absolved of the sin of stealing off with Florissa? Emma's presence surely legitimized the poet's return did it not? But Simon failed to introduce her; and as it was, Sir Anthony continued to take no particular notice of her. Instead his eyes darted frantically about like those of a weasel caught in a trap.

"I say, Chase," Simon persisted, taking the liberty of clapping the other man heartily on the back, causing him to shrink back as if he had been pawed by a leper. "I'm just back from Italy, you know. Bit out of touch with the happenings in town. What's on the docket for tonight? Anything at Prinny's?"

"Oh, tonight," Chase demurred, his color turning ashy. "Tonight, is it? Tonight? Prinny's. No, nothing much on tonight."

Despite the almost pitiful eagerness to depart which Chase barely attempted to disguise, Simon would not release the squat pink, green, and yellow bird, and Emma's discomfort forced her, finally, to look away toward the crowd. But a still more unpleasant scene awaited her there. Even to her squinting, uncertain gaze it was clear that everyone's fullest attention was turned upon them. How could even she overlook the whispers, the stares, even a giggle or two? The whole *ton* was watching, but not approaching, and certainly not approving. When, in despair, she turned her gaze once more to her companions, it was only to find Simon still holding fast to his prisoner, whose agony had grown so fevered that he was forced to whip a mauve damask handkerchief out of his pocket and mop his brow.

Escape was now entirely out of the question for the large beau; but, so desperate was he to elude Jason's grasp, that he actually turned toward the less scandalous member of the pair. "Madame," he addressed Emma for the first time, "I don't believe I've had the honor of making your acquaintance."

And suddenly Simon leaped in again, "I say, Anthony, haven't you met Emma Davenant?"

It was perhaps this final straw that stripped all semblance of good manners from Sir Anthony. The beau purpled, and could not manage to repress a strangled, "Oh, no, not the cousin!"

The moment of speechlessness following this outburst allowed for Chase to make good an escape. "Ah!" he called, as he began to ease away, "there's Arabella Portney and her sister Caroline! Must to them at once. Promised to meet them half an hour ago."

And off he would have bolted had not a new figure strode directly into their midst, exclaiming, "Simon Herbert! Good to see you!" Although Sir Anthony had already turned away from his captors, he now halted uncertainly. Torn between the exhilaration of freedom and the fatal curiosity of the *ton*, he was unsure whether he ought to risk the danger of recapture simply to learn who dared greet the pariah in so familiar and jolly a fashion.

Having decided in favor of the *ton*, he wheeled slowly around to find himself facing the illustrious Beau Leicester. Poor fella, must have caught some sort of brain fever in the tropics, Chase surmised, else why in the world would he greet that wretched Jason as if they were old school chums?

But, as it turned out, that was not to be the most stunning development. For now the dazzling Beau turned his justly renowned eyes on that mouse of a girl, seized her hand, and—for God's sake!—proceeded to kiss it before speaking warmly to her. "Lady Emma! There is no one I'd rather see at the Serpentine! And looking so charming, too."

Sir Anthony suddenly was uncomfortably aware that Leicester hadn't acknowledged him. Might he not? Did he mean to cut him? To be ignored by the Beau in favor of that vile poet fella and that little nobody would mean permanent disgrace before the world. Therefore he screwed up his courage and thrust his hand at Leicester, who, blessedly, dropped the girl's and accepted his. Although the grasp was not so enthusiastic as Sir Anthony might have wished, it was firm enough to get him off the hook— or so it seemed, until the Beau addressed him. "Chase, I hear there's going to be the deuce of a party at Prinny's tonight. Are you going?"

Sir Anthony had no recourse but to mutter, "Yes."

"Ah, then," Leicester continued, "we'll see you there. Lady Emma has consented to accompany me, and we have urged Lord Jason to join our party. But now," he turned his attention to his companions, "I must be off. *Will* you be joining us, Lord Jason?"

Jason nodded, beaming, as Emma stared at Marcus, speechless with disbelief at this second miraculous visitation by her rented Lord Cupid.

"Come on, you two," Leicester urged them breezily. "I'll walk you back to the carriage, and on the way we'll make arrangements for tonight."

The three of them bid a jaunty farewell to Sir Anthony, glued to the very spot he would previously have given a fortune to be quit of. And he was not the only one struck dumb. The entire *ton*, having witnessed the intrusion of the unprecedented into this vale of conformity, had turned quite to salt.

And, as Leicester drove back to Chelsea, leaving a glowing Emma in the dubious care of her preening ebony peacock, he blessed the instinct which always alerted him when a lady needed help. For it was surely instinct and nothing else which had impelled him to quit Cheyne Walk and rush toward the Serpentine to rescue a damsel in distress.

Chapter VI

UPON PARTING FROM the happy couple at the Serpentine, the cupid in gabardine had informed Lady Emma that he would come round to Belgrave Square at tenish to conduct her and her swain to Carleton House. And so it was with some astonishment that Emma received, at barely seven, the announcement of Leicester's arrival. But the small annoyance she may have felt at the unexpected intrusion upon her private meditations was far outstripped by her relief at being spared the solitary agony of deciding what to wear.

That relief turned quickly to shock, however, when, preparing to descend to the jade drawing room, Emma was interrupted by the manifestation in her doorway of the cupid himself.

"May I come in?" Casually propping one evening-suited shoulder against the doorframe, Marcus waited for Emma to recover from the curious reaction so often evoked in women viewing him for the first time in full evening clothes. Long ago he had ceased puzzling over the phenomenon and learned to accept the fact that for some minute or so after he presented himself to a woman in the black gabardine suit with satin lapels that he and Brummell had devised, she would indubitably fall into a sort of standing swoon. Speechless, staring, stupefied. Certainly there was no danger: it lasted only a moment. They had all recovered, just as Emma was already beginning to.

Only when her hand had flown to quiet her pounding heart did Emma recall that, while the cupid was garbed like a prince in a fairy tale, she was the perfect picture of a scullery maid or, worse yet, a mad girl. Not only was her hair a veritable tangle of serpents, but she was clad in the poor, ruined dressing gown she could not bring herself to put down, despite the fact that the blue velvet had not been anything near royal for many years while the elbows were worn through and the hem dragged in the back. And, as if all that were not enough, the ribbons originally intended to be tied into bows to hold it closed had long ago shredded to nothingness, permitting an almost uninterrupted view of Emma's chemise. But sorriest of all, far worse even than her shabby *déshabille*, were her spectacles.

Although half-emerged from the trance into which she had been cast by Leicester's appearance, Emma was still so stunned by her own embarrassment that she had not yet recovered her powers of speech, hearing, and movement.

Marcus had studied the syndrome long enough to be proficient in administering the antidote. Taking the liberty of entering the lady's drawing room without permission, he crossed to her, took one chilled hand in his, gazed deeply into her heavily misted eyes, and shouted her name.

"Lady Emma!" Slowly her glance began to clear, then her head moved ever so slightly, and her right hand per-

44

ceptibly loosed its deathlike grip on the bodice of her dressing gown. Finally she murmured, "Lord Leicester! You surprised me!" Her eyes were gliding, as if with a will of their own, from the black satin cravat stuck with a diamond pin, over the wide, shining lapel crowned with a white carnation, to the precipitous edge of the straight, wide shoulders. They ran down the perfect creaseless length of one black gabardine sleeve to the snowy white cuff delicately edging the long, graceful hand that still held hers. The sight of her own fingers retained exquisitely in that alluringly open palm succeeded where his words could not: with a tiny step backward, she relieved his hand of hers, which she sent straight to join the other on the open bosom of her dressing gown.

"Call me Marcus." He smiled with an easy grin as he strolled over to a blue-and-white striped love seat and made himself comfortable.

Ignoring his suggestion, she commenced her interrogation. "Lord Leicester, what has become of Harsant? Where are the servants? Why are you not still in the jade drawing room? And is it not just seven?"

"Ah," he replied jovially, "I'll answer your queries only on three conditions: one, that you call me Marcus; two, that you consent to sit down; and, three, that you dispense with your embarrassment at being surprised in your pet dressing gown. I grew up with three sisters and have seen women dressed in even stranger fashion."

Which fact Emma had never doubted. Still his words served to put her somewhat at ease, and she duly consented to the aforenamed conditions.

Arranging the tatters of her dressing gown as elegantly as possible in a gray silk armchair, she smiled weakly and pursued, "Did you not have an engagement for dinner tonight?"

"Yes, but it was with my friend Brummell, whom I see

quite frequently enough. The Carleton House situation, to my mind, outweighed in urgency an appointment easily rearranged."

"Yes?" Again she was stunned.

"Yes, indeed. I have come three hours before Lord Jason to commence our program of study *sub rosa*, and *tout de suite* . . ."

The smile he expected to greet this witticism was never to be born. Instead he found to his dismay that the lady's only response was a slight steeling of her previously bemisted gaze. "What?"

"Lady Emma," he persevered more cheerily than ever, "I intend to commence our first lesson right now!" He absolutely beamed with what she assumed to be professional *bonhomie*. "To answer your question about the servants. Upon your butler's invitation to escort me to the jade drawing room, I seized the opportunity to enlist his confidence in our little enterprise.

"Oh, no!" he interjected as he saw her blanch. "Banish the notion, Lady Emma, that we can conduct this programme without the servant's complicity. Banish the notion." She intuited, for the first time, a certain obdurateness in his tone which warned her to let the objection pass. And, indeed, her silence seemed to please him, for she could detect a general brightening of his manner. "Good," he responded sunnily. "Now, to continue, Harsant has been dispatched to the kitchen, to inform Cook that dinner will be served up here. Mrs. Gillings and the little maid, Lucy, are presently bringing some equipment from my carriage to your chambers and should arrive in this very doorway at any moment."

And, of course, no sooner had the magus completed his incantation, than first Gillings and then Lucy materialized, staggering under the weight of strange devices and multicolored boxes of all sizes and shapes.

"Ah, ladies!" Marcus had risen to his feet and strolled to the bedroom door. "Take 'em right through there. Throw 'em all on the bed for the time being." Relieving the ladies of the bulk of their burdens, Marcus proceeded to allow them into the chamber to deposit the heavy artillery.

Despite the storm of activity that raged around her, Emma remained rooted to her seat, wracked by multitudinous uncertainties, chief among them being the correct demeanor for entertaining in her bedchamber a man other than her father. But her quandary was resolved almost at once, when Marcus poked his head through the bedroom doorway and called out impatiently, "Lady Emma. Time is wasting! Will you join us!" And she did, trembling at the prospect of the unknown destiny awaiting her in her own bedchamber.

The bedroom had blossomed, in seconds, into a lady's meadow, running riot with rose silks, orchid satins, and gardenia velvets, brilliant with shimmering ponds of jewels, and lush with groves of ermine tails. This gorgeous *jardin* was so richly overgrown that the bed beneath it had no more substance to the eye than the brown earth of a posy-covered field. And bordering the field, like a kitchen garden, sprouted hedges of boxes, bottles, pots, flasks, brushes, combs, puffs, curling irons, stockings, slippers, gloves, reticules of every design, needles of all sizes and threads of all hues. The wardrobe doors had been flung open, and, at Marcus's command, his two good soldiers were extracting garments for his judgment.

Emma, wandering through the garden which had sprung up where her bedroom used to be, thought to swoon with the shock, but decided against it; her teacher had assumed so military a command over the engagement that, should she faint, she might just wake some small time later, to find herself dressed from head to foot, having given no

47

more consent than a doll would. Once again, the question of Leicester's salary flitted through her mind. How vast must it be to provoke a servant to such an excess of dutifulness?

Finding herself before a tiny bare section of the bed, she began to sink down upon it when she was interrupted by the stentorian tones of her tutor-torturer: "Don't bother to sit down, Lady Emma. We have much to accomplish and little time. Go over there, behind the screen. That's the girl. Right over there." She hesitantly followed his gesture to the appointed spot. "Now, lower your hands from your dressing gown." Above the gilded frame of the blue brocade screen, appeared two spectacled and terrified eyes topped by a tangled nest of auburn curls. "Have you lowered your hands?" he persisted maddeningly. After a pause the curls bobbed in silent response. "Good. Now, remove the dressing gown and sling it over the screen in front of you." To his own secret mild surprise, she obeyed.

Above the screen the two frightened eyes reappeared, tensed for the next command; but, when it was delivered, it was not to them. "Lucy, convey to Lady Emma the apple-green underfrock and assist her in assuming it." Lucy, only just regaining the composure she had lost to the sight of Beau Leicester in evening clothes, came instantly to life, seizing up the dress and joining her mistress behind the screen.

"Oh, ma'am!" the perky little maid took the liberty of whispering in a tone sufficiently hushed for the confessional, "he's the handsomest gentleman I ever seen!" This disclosure provoked only a smothered response from the mistress, swathed as she was in the yards of pale green silk presently bunched over her head. "I swear," the indefatigably enthusiastic girl burbled on, "when I first beheld 'im in them evenin' clothes, I nearly took a swoon! And so did Miss Gillings, no matter what she tells you!" Once

Emma's adornment was completed, there was no more rustling silk to camouflage confidences, and the chattering soliloquy ceased. Only a few more hooks needed hooking, and then both girls stood at attention, awaiting their orders.

"All right, Lady Emma, now come around the screen, come right around like that," Marcus drawled. She first poked her head out, then slowly crept from her hiding place. "Now walk over to the mirror, just walk over there." Like a failed suicide, hauled betimes from the river of luxury, she trembled with the cold of submission and crossed to the mirror in a humble posture of defeat. "Now, turn so that you *face* the mirror. And step back a few paces so you can see yourself properly." She was in the process of doing so when Harsant appeared, followed by Cook, both bearing huge, covered trays from which emanated the fragrant smells of dinner.

Dinner! As if to announce its mistress's neglect of it since the morning hours, Emma's stomach chose that moment to growl. And only then did she realize she had eaten almost nothing at breakfast and had taken no food since that time. She was starving, and the sight of Cook and Harsant laying a small inlaid table with the exquisite feast caused her head veritably to swim. She had started blindly toward her object, when the tutor's firm voice once again halted her progress. "Lady Emma, first things first. You have the rest of your life for dinner, but only a few hours until Lord Jason arrives. Believe me, your time will be better spent costuming yourself for tonight's event."

"He's right, milady," chimed in Cook, not even bothering to raise her head from the duck with figs which she was presently carving up. "And, besides," considered the gruff but kindly little lady, "you wouldn't want your dress to fit tighter than it has to, ma'am. Always better to skip your dinner and wait until midnight supper."

Emma had never previously suspected Cook's interest in

or knowledge of the *ton*, but instinct told the mistress to trust the servant's advice. Still she could not help but feel the slightest resentment at Cook's painstaking attention to the service of the dazzling figure in evening clothes. While Emma stood lost, hungry, and fuming, Cook urged one elaborate dish after another upon Marcus, Harsant standing at the ready with a different wine for every course.

The cursed Beau, of course, responded by displaying the most enthusiastic yet discriminating of appetites. No praise was too great for the Scotch salmon mousse, no adjective hyperbole for the duckling. Never 'til this moment had Brussels sprouts of such perfection passed his lips, and (with a nod toward Harsant) the claret was, quite simply, first rate.

Now Beau Leicester glanced up from his plate, idly twirled his wineglass, and directed at least a portion of his concentration to the half-starved Emma. "Do not be distracted by my dining, Lady Emma," he offered, setting down the glass and taking up again his knife and fork, "for I shall not be. I have made it a practice always to try to do two things at once." His smile drew the same response from Emma as it did from the duckling under his knife.

"Harumph," he continued, "I have been wondering, ma'am, why it is that, given your auburn coloring, I find such a profusion of blues and burgundies in your wardrobe. Moreover, from only a quick perusal, I have gathered that you possess a proclivity for gowns designed for a female form somewhat fuller than your own. I cannot understand why this should be. It is as if your gowns were made with someone else in mind."

The frank suggestion of her fledgling instructor stung her, as unpleasant truths are wont to.

"How very perceptive of you, Lord Leicester," she congratulated him, the lightness of tone barely covering her shame at being such a goose. "In point of fact," she continued bravely, "most of those gowns *were* purchased under the direction of another lady, whose coloring and height are quite different from mine. Perhaps she found it difficult to judge what would flatter a smaller, slighter shape."

Or perhaps, Marcus thought, if it was Florissa de Coucy of whom Emma spoke, the lady in question had simply not given a damn about Emma's particular requirements. It must, then, have been the fabulous Florissa who had decorated the house to flatter herself—hence, the burgundy saloon, Emma's blue bedroom, the awful-hued gowns cut in the wrong shape. Florissa had made the house her own showcase, and all at poor Emma's expense. God, the woman was a vixen! And shameless, to boot. All that, and then to run off with the poor girl's beau!

What a dreadful string of luck Emma Davenant had enjoyed. And that was to be regretted, despite the fact that, although he was not yet sure how, he was positive Emma had contributed to her own misfortune. But her luck would surely turn now. With the help of the Creator he would do his utmost to see to it.

He returned to the subject herself. "Now, this little gown you are presently wearing. What is its provenance?"

He was studying her studying herself in the mirror, and the reflection of their eyes met and held in the glass. "I . . . ," she murmured, "I . . . I picked it out myself. About six months ago. But Flor—but the other lady pronounced it too plain and dull-hued."

"Nonsense; you displayed excellent taste in the purchase," he countered. "Compare your appearance in this gown to that of the costume you wore when we first met. Whereas that dress was overpowering for a figure so petite as yours, this little green frock is cut with such economy of line and tone that, rather than diminishing, it enhances your shape and your coloring. Observe.''

In the mirror his eyes traced her form, inviting her to follow. "See how the width and depth of the neckline serve to highlight the creaminess of your skin, as well as the length of your neck—a superb feature in a woman— and the grace of your shoulders.''

Even in the mirror his professional, albeit caressing examination threatened to bring a blush to that creamy skin. And the risk increased, for now his eyes traced a light path to her waist, where they lingered.

He briskly resumed his commentary. "Though some might call your figure boyish''—she paled—"I feel that such a form as yours is very well suited to the simple, elegant lines of a modern gown such as this. Whilst our more, umm, robust mamas and grandmamas might prefer flounces and layers, those times have passed. And you are blessed with a figure for today's fashions.''

He ignored her hesitant smile of gratitude and contin- ued, "Let's try those little ivory kid slippers . . . Gill- ings, those, yes, the fifth pair down the row! Perfect. And, Lucy, the matching long gloves. Yes, very fetching with the tiny sleeves. Good arms! You should feature them.''

Despite the demands of his work Marcus had managed, between breaths, to consume his entire dinner, never once talking with a full mouth. Now he downed the last of his claret, pushed back the chair, and rose, still gazing at her gazing at him in the glass. Slowly, very slowly, he crossed to her and stopped some eight or so inches behind her. More slowly still, his hands rose toward the arms he had called good, toward the shoulders he had praised for their grace, moving ever closer as he softly suggested, "Now let's try the forest green overdress! I believe I've guessed your measurements correctly. Gillings!''

And, as he accepted the garment and helped her into it,

as his fingers grazed her skin, Emma felt the faintest breath of a clear and present danger in the room.

The ormolu chinoiserie clock had struck ten some twenty minutes past, but the grouping in the jade drawing room remained incomplete. Having been bathed and coiffed and *maquillaged*, then hemmed and hooked up like a dressmaker's dummy, Emma was fatigued and even more famished and undeniably disappointed that the man of her thoughts had not rushed to her side at ten sharp.

It had been over half an hour ago that she descended the staircase on Marcus's arm, "bending almost imperceptibly toward her partner," as Leicester had instructed her. And once inside the confines of the jade drawing room, the Beau had arranged her perfectly along a green-and-white striped *chaise longue* to resemble, however faintly, the exquisite Madame Récamier of David. But, as the interminable moments dragged by without the appearance of the swain, Emma felt her carefully prepared dewiness begin to evaporate; in her mood's sky rose the red sun of irritation.

"Lord Leicester," she commenced after a long mutual silence which acknowledged that the only sound worth hearing was the front doorbell.

"*Marcus*," came the retort, but soon it was followed by a more measured explication. "Lady Emma, it is most important that you call me Marcus. You will impress the world of a . . . a certain intimacy between us. You take my meaning?"

"Completely," she snapped back, proceeding then to edge her foot, which had fallen asleep, off the couch. "But I'm *starving*," she wailed and made her leap to freedom, landing, unfortunately, on the slumbering foot, and plunging to the floor in a pool of green velvet and silk.

Flying at once to her side, Marcus helped her up, placed her once more on the couch, and dropped to his knees before her. Then, without a moment's hesitation, he removed her shoe and began to stroke the senseless extremity back into life.

"It hurts!" Emma shrieked; as infinite tiny bee stings assaulted her poor numb limb; but his touch was firm and knowing, and the agony soon faded. Her head was bent over his, as he bent over the foot which his massage had now restored to exquisite sensitivity. The crisis past, Emma was suddenly all too aware of the continuing pleasure of the touch of his hand. "Umm," she murmured. Well, she would order him to stop in, oh, just another moment or two. Just another moment of him, kneeling before her, softly kneading her instep, stroking her ankle and her calf. Just one more moment, and she would open her eyes. . . .

But when she did, her first clear vision was of a lone figure standing in the doorway. It was Lord Jason, and his face could have passed for the deathmask of a man struck down by shock.

For an inestimable second that same shock held the lady on the couch in its thrall, and the room in silent suspension. But then, as at the flick of a magician's wand, the scene animated. Marcus, still bent over Emma, was the only character unconscious of the little drama about to unfold, until Emma's sudden retraction of her foot warned him that something was amiss.

As he raised his glance to her countenance, he was surprised to find it bore an expression of terror, as if induced by some horrifying presence behind him. As he was turning his head to confront the terrible apparition, Emma began to address it. She had gotten only so far as "Lord Jason, let me ex—" when Marcus bolted (albeit with infinite grace) to his feet, his back to her, blocking her view of the frozen poet in the doorway. But still she persevered: "It was . . . oh! my *foot*."

Her words had been intended to clear the air, but they

were largely drowned out by a sudden fit of coughing on the part of Lord Leicester, and then utterly halted by the painfully sharp weight of Marcus's foot on her own recently revived one. It continued to press its message home as Lord Jason opened his mouth to speak.

"Your *foot*? Did you say your foot?" Simon demanded from the outer ring of confusion.

"My *foot*?" Emma responded rather loftily. "Why, Simon, whatever can you be speaking of?"

At Emma's completion of this perfectly turned phrase, Marcus obligingly released her foot from beneath his and walked across the room, seating himself with consummate ease and drawing out a cigarette from a handsome ebony case.

Emma, meanwhile, was bending down in an attempt to locate her shoe, all the while fixing her eyes upon Simon, whose glance shifted anxiously back and forth from the lady to the Beau, searching for some clue as to what had transpired.

When that quest produced nothing, he cautiously entered the room, moved to Emma, fell to his knees, and gingerly kissed her hand. Lowering his voice to simulate privacy, he murmured, "Emma! How very lovely you are tonight."

And, indeed, she was. It was to Admiral Davenant's great credit that he had chosen so expert and uncompromising an instructor for his only daughter; but it must be said that Marcus had truly outdone himself. Whereas that morning Emma had appeared too much like a doll outfitted by an overzealous little girl, tonight she was turned out with such elegant simplicity that her presence advertised the virtues of pure prettiness.

The apple green of her underdress shimmered with a delicacy that contrasted delightfully with the deep, rich hue of the exquisitely unadorned overdress. Aside from the long kid gloves, Marcus had ordered that decoration be kept to

55

a minimum, in accordance with the latest fashion, and she wore no jewelry save tiny pearldrop earrings and a thin gold chain at the throat.

Gillings having been shifted to wardrobe, the crucial duties of coiffure and *maquillage* had fallen to the surprisingly adept Lucy. Consequently Emma's recalcitrant hair had at last been properly subdued, and rolled, twisted, and twirled into a semblance of spontaneity that could only have resulted from arduous hours before the mirror. The brilliant auburn of her tresses glowed against the cream of her skin and the lush greens of her gown, and, with the correct lightness of touch, Lucy had applied rouge to her mistress's cheeks and lips to suggest only the natural glow of unabashed youth.

As her gaze danced from the top of Simon's head to Marcus, Emma was surprised to observe the long, thick eyelashes descending over one blue-gray eye in what only could be described as a wink. Although that unexpected action provoked in her an almost irresistible desire to giggle, she restrained herself. Instead, she addressed herself to the suitor at her feet. "And you, Simon, you look splendid."

The poet, like the Beau, was dressed in black, but not in Leicester's fashion. Rather his evening costume echoed that in which he had first appeared, although the daytime serges and cottons had been replaced by ebony satins, velvets, and silks, and his cravatless shirt glowed the color of cream. Over all of this, he had slung a most elegant cape bordered solemnly in sable, but lined in dazzling crimson. Unlike the patent leather slippers which adorned the feet of the great Beau, fitting neatly under the satin-striped trousers of his dinner clothes, Simon's high-heeled pumps were topped by a long expanse of black stocking-clad leg. His fair curls were arranged in a most elaborate fashion, and his cologne promised hours of maidenly rapture.

Gazing down upon him, Emma was forced to compare the poet with the gentleman who had until this very moment captured her thoughts along with her wardrobe. Leicester's demeanor, not unlike his countenance, was flawless, perfectly poised, and his luminous eyes met hers with a clarity suggesting all honesty of intent. Simon's, on the other hand, startling in their icy opacity, bespoke intellect masking a too long restrained passion. Clearly Marcus Leicester's eyes were the eyes of natural, easy elegance while Simon Herbert's were the orbs of a pained sort of genius.

From their early awkward meetings and their hesitant conversation, Emma had intuited a great gift lurking behind Simon's mumbled phrases and sullen silences. And when, in the first flush of their fumbling friendship, he had begun to show her his poem, and then to admit her to its inner workings, her admiration for the poet he would someday be grew along with a helpless fondness for his boyish rudeness and lack of grace. Always he had responded to her praise, with a manner so promising of rapture, so frank in its admission of his need for her, that she had come to love their passionate future at the expense of their disaffected present. He would someday be great, and she would be beside him, stroking the golden curls, as he showered her with an adoration that would melt those icy blue eyes.

As she now detected in him that same irresistible promise of passion, softened a bit by his newly penitential air, Emma's heart allowed itself a merry leap. He was here, and she was happy. Lifting her head with a new elegance the cupid had already instilled in her, she turned her gaze back to that instructor and proceeded to return his wink.

"And now," announced the cupid in question, "it's time to be off," and he rose, motioning Emma to do the same.

Bidding Simon rise to his feet, she allowed him to help her up and to retain her arm, bending almost inperceptibly toward him, as they passed, with Marcus close behind, out the door and on to Carleton House.

Chapter VII

BEHIND HER SHONE the glamorous thoroughfare that was Pall Mall. Before her the grand staircase of Carleton House rose in awesome prospect.

This was not the first time that Emma had stood at the bottom of the *ton*'s ladder to heaven, but her previous encounters had been fraught with breathless trepidation and an escalation of her nervousness to the sheerest terror. Now with not one, but two, devoted escorts at her side, she felt her stomach flutter only once, before it was soothed by the new possibility of pleasure.

Along the curving upward spiral, great bouquets of blossoms, like jewels set in a coiffure, glowed in perfect brilliance. And at the summit, through the ballroom's open doors, the sounds of music and laughter burst forth.

In a rare gesture of general largesse, Simon had offered to see to the wraps of the party. As the poet dispatched himself to the cloakroom, Marcus determined to take advantage of their moment of solitude to equip Emma with brief but salient instruction.

Seizing her hand with totally convincing ardor, the Beau escorted Emma to a marble bench against one wall and begged her to be seated. Once she was thus ensconced, Marcus proceeded to seat himself closer to her than the size of the bench seemed to require. As if that were not enough, he began at once to whisper in her ear, to the amazement both of the assembled company, and of Emma herself.

But, instead of the words of endearment which any observer would have vowed to be the single business of so gallant a swain, Marcus hissed urgently, "Lady Emma, do not forget. You must appear to have a *tendre* for me, and I for you. Just you follow where I lead, and you will see how quickly Lord Jason's manners will improve." And he sealed the secret message with a gentle kiss to the hand, obvious both to the passersby and to the returning Simon. Only at the last moment did Marcus appear to notice the poet's approach, at which time he sprang back from the lady, precipitously dropping her hand.

"Have I interrupted you?" Simon asked with a determination that bespoke his intention not to absent himself again.

"Not in the least," Marcus contributed, his levity seeming rather forced. "Far from it, old fellow. Well, shall we?" And he immediately took Emma's hand again and led her up the wide staircase, while disconcerted Simon followed in his wake.

The ballroom glittered with the light of more candles than one might ever count, their ornate chandeliers somehow effortlessly suspended high in the heavens beneath the lofty ceiling. Huge windows opened out onto a balcony from which could be viewed the lavish expanse of Piccadilly, affording a gentle spring breeze to cool the elegant throng within. The gold-and-wood inlaid walls, the exquisite marble friezes above, the show of *ton*, laughter and conversation below: withal, it presented an extraordinary picture of glamour and gracious delight. The music and dancing, which had already begun when our trio entered the room, completed this *tableau vivant*; and their entrance froze it.

Although Beau Leicester had been seen only briefly that afternoon at the Serpentine, news of his return to London had sped through the *ton*, and many a lady had devoted an additional hour or more to her evening's toilette. The gentlemen, too, even the Prince Regent, distressed by the possibility of paling in the comparison, had dressed to the nines. All in all, Prinny's palace had never shone quite so fabulously as it did that night.

And, as Emma entered the ballroom on Marcus's arm, she found that the entire company's attention was directed, by association, to her. Every step, every gesture of the great Beau and his fair companion were closely studied. Even those few toffs who knew Emma failed to recognize her in her renovated state, and more than one of them questioned his companion about the fresh and lovely lady on Leicester's arm.

The ladies, on the other hand, struck with the disappointment that Marcus Leicester had come committed, said nothing at all; but they stored away every scrap of perception and each unspoken remark for the next morning when, gathered together, they would begin to piece together their recollections of the woman's behavior into a patchwork of flaws, faults, and gracelessnesses.

Whilst Emma was acutely aware of this attentive observation, Marcus seemed not even to notice. He devoted himself entirely to her, as if they were alone together in the jade drawing room in Belgrave Square, nodding occasionally to a familiar face as he walked with her through the watchful crowd.

"May I fetch you some refreshment, Lady Emma?" he inquired, smiling warmly, and whispering under his breath, "You're doing fine." Turning to the still trailing Simon, he politely repeated his offer.

Simon, having decided not to make the same mistake twice, replied rather sullenly, "A little *porto*," without moving so much as an inch.

"And you, Lady Emma, what will you have?" Marcus pursued.

Smiling as beguilingly as she could, Emma deliberated a moment before responding, "I can't think what I would like. You choose," she cooed, allowing herself a moment's pause before adding meaningfully, ". . . Marcus," and she was pleased to see Simon pale before this new hint of intimacy.

"I think, Lady Emma," Marcus suggested, "that a strawberry ratafia would be the perfect refreshment. Let me go see to it." Bowing slightly, he departed her side to search out a servingman.

Left briefly alone with the suddenly glamorous lady, Simon was clearly disturbed by Emma's unanticipated ascension. Granted, she had never been lovelier than tonight; but how to explain Beau Leicester's great infatuation with the little thing? There had to be more to it than love at first sight. But what? Damn that Leicester. Just like him to arrive in the nick of time to throw Simon's own grand plans into jeopardy! But at least he could use the time until Leicester returned to regain his lost footing. He moved closer to Emma and, taking both her hands in his, murmured, "Emma, we have so much to talk of, you and I." Lowering her lashes in an unexpected act of coquetry, Emma replied, smiling only a little, "I wonder what can be keeping Marcus."

The poet's irritation at being ignored could no longer be

contained. "Keeping him? My God, Emma, he's only been gone for two minutes."

"Oh?" she replied, allowing her voice to drift off into utter dreaminess. "It seems so much longer," and Simon's ice-blue eyes turned to steel.

Just at that moment Marcus reappeared, all smiles and solicitousness. "Done," he announced, his eyes on Emma. "The refreshments will be here momentarily." And, following fast upon his words, a liveried servant materialized, bearing a silver tray with three glasses. "The ratafia for the lady," Marcus indicated, gracefully placing the glass in her hand. "And the *porto* for the gentleman." Allowing Simon to serve himself, the Beau seized up his own glass of mysterious golden liquid.

"May I ask what it is you are drinking?" Simon inquired with only an undertone of resentment.

"Ah, this." Marcus examined the glass. "A peculiarity of mine, I confess. Discovered it in Scotland some few years past. Called whiskey. They stock it here for me. Would you like to try it?"

Simon did his best to turn up his nose. "No thanks. I'll stick with the *porto*."

Emma, desperately grateful for the taste of something, had downed the ratafia in one gulp, and now boldly announced, "I'd like to try . . . what do you call it? Whiskey?"

A flash of concern emanated from the gray-blue eyes. "Are you sure, Lady Emma? It's really quite strong."

"I am quite sure, Lor—, Marcus." She stated her will with great deliberateness, then turned to the waiter. "Bring me a whiskey."

"Very good, milady," the servant tonelessly assented, and went off to get it.

In seconds the waiter had reappeared, bearing a tray on which rested a single glass. This time Simon hastened to assure himself of the honor of handing Emma the whiskey, after first going so far as to remove her own empty glass from her grasp to replace it on the tray. The lady smiled slightly at his sudden attentiveness, then raised the glass to her lips and sipped.

After the sweet, rich ratafia, Emma was in no way prepared for the bitter fire which blazed down her throat. Only to herself would she confess that she had never tasted so noxious a preparation since the times of early childhood illness.

To her audience she murmured, "Quite good," and forced another sip down her throat, wondering all the while what a man of the world like Marcus saw in the beverage, but bestowing on the Beau the most sincere of pleasurable glances. Although she suspected she saw some doubt in his eyes, she continued to play her part, and when Marcus had downed the foul brew and ordered another, she followed suit. Now Marcus's disapproval became more evident.

"Lady Emma," he insisted, "I advise you not to—"

"Nonsense," Simon unexpectedly broke in. "The lady wants another whiskey, and she shall have it." The last remark was addressed with a new firmness to the serving-man, who nevertheless looked to Marcus for instructions. Receiving a silent shrug from that quarter, the servant hurried off for the second round.

"My, isn't it warm in here?" Emma, of a sudden, felt as if she were running a fever. In fact, she wondered if she were not coming down with the *ague*, for, in addition to her fevered state, she was becoming slightly dizzy, and for some strange reason, giddy as well, feeling an almost irresistible urge to giggle. But, attributing her curious condition to all the excitement of the last day and the fact that she had not eaten, she decided it would pass and thought to disguise it behind a veneer of sophistication.

From somewhere at once very close and far away she heard Marcus's voice suggesting the cool relief of the terrace, and allowed herself to be held gently by the elbow and steered through the French doors. Since Simon had lingered behind to direct the waiter to their new station, Marcus took advantage of their few private moments to state with some urgency, "Lady Emma, I beg you, no more whiskey. I intuit that you are not feeling well, and that may well be the cause."

But Emma, cheered by the night breeze into the most assertive of good humors, did not fail to oppose him. "Lord Leicester . . . No, Marcus." For some inexplicable reason she found that notion too amusing not to giggle over. "Marcus," she repeated, as if she were trying to memorize his name, and giggled again.

"Emma!" Overlooking the real urgency and concern in his tone, she could not help but focus on the fact that he had left off the "Lady," nor could she subdue the broad, even dazzling smile she now flashed upon him. "Marcus," she beamed as she drew herself up to her full height, which still left the distance of a foot between their eyes, "I am a grown woman and am able to make certain decisions without advice."

"Ah, here you are," Simon cried as he bounded onto the terrace, followed by the waiter, who dispensed the beverages and retired. Although Marcus slowly sipped the second whiskey, his student once more drained off the brew in an instant. Then, thinking to place the delicate crystal on the balcony railing, she overestimated its width and set the glass down on the thin air, through which it fell to splinters on the road far below. Emma laughed delightedly.

Suddenly her attention was caught by the music wafting from the ballroom. "Oh," she exclaimed merrily, "the waltz. How I should love to dance this dance!"

"But, Emma," the poet interrupted, "you don't waltz."

"Oh yes I do, don't I, Marcus?" and she turned to her savior.

The Beau, of course, had taught all manner of women, from small girls to grandmothers, to waltz, but heretofore had never instructed a tipsy one. Still the exercise might bring her around, if he could just keep her on her feet.

"Of course, Lady Emma," he graciously agreed. "My great pleasure." And in they went to commence the dancing lesson.

Chapter VIII

THE RECENT WHISKEY giddiness had done nothing in aid of Emma's unspectacled state; even under Marcus's expert captaincy, she managed, as they prepared to reenter the ballroom, to veer just enough to walk directly into a French door. Luckily Marcus's eye was as quick as his arm was strong, and he managed to steer her back on course before the misstep was perceptible to any observer.

Just as they passed out of the terrace, a breeze arose and danced mercurially past them into the ballroom, like a young girl running to meet her favorite partner. Moments ago the orchestra had struck up the latest Viennese confection, and the dazzling couples, men in Marcus's black, women in every color of the universe, strolled to the dance floor and drew together.

Anne Gillings had lectured Emma endlessly on the dangers inherent in a man holding a woman in public, but the warnings had failed to penetrate Emma's imagination, and it was to the waltz that all her daydreams dipped and spun. Still, along with the spring breeze had come the cold wind of self-consciousness which brought Emma around just enough to acknowledge that, truly, she did not waltz. Or, rather, she had not waltzed. But, then, she had never before had Marcus as a partner. Since he could so brilliantly play Pygmalion to her Galatea, perhaps the role of Terpsichore would prove no more impossible a challenge.

Alas her doubt grew, for even to her uncertain vision, each couple beginning to circle the room seemed perfectly graceful, perfectly flawless. Once again she was shaken by the prospect of executing those infinite, intricate steps, and disbelieved in the seemingly magical transformation of two pairs of feet into one.

What had provoked her to risk such awful public humiliation? She who early on in life had displayed an absolute inability to follow anything or anyone, much less Marcus Leicester to the center of Carleton House. As he escorted her toward the whirling dancers, Emma instinctively drew back, and Marcus sensed it. "Lady Emma," he whispered gently, making sure not to loosen his grip on her unsteady elbow, "you demur."

Even as her heart pounded with dread, she realized she had proceeded too far to retreat, and, resigning herself to a fate far worse than death, she drew her breath in sharply and replied, "By no means, Marcus!" She turned and gave him what was intended to be her most fearless smile. He grinned in return, then took her hand and led her into the thick of the glamorous carousel.

"Well, here we go!" Elegantly courageous, he positioned her opposite him and, before she could teeter, deftly wrapped an arm about her and drew her close until perilously little space separated them.

He inclined his head in the general direction of her ear, presenting to any onlooker the impression that he breathed sweet nothings into it, and instructed in a low whisper, "Now put your arm loosely around me, as I have done to you; yes, right around me. Excellent. Now I shall take your hand in mine," doing so as he spoke. "And now, the most important thing of all: as soon as I have completed these words, feign a sort of swooning and fall backward into my arm. Don't worry, I won't drop you; but you must make sure to let yourself go and follow my lead. Remember, as if you were swooning."

Had she been somewhat less dizzy, had she been clearer-headed and quite herself, she would have allowed her numberless fears to overwhelm and paralyze her. As it was, the tipsy Emma immediately found her courage and fell backward into what she otherwise would have realized to be irredeemable humiliation. Imagine her surprise when her certain ruin was prevented by the rapturous impediment of his firm arm, which held her fast. Smiling with infinite charm, he murmured, "Shall we dance?" and they began.

Afterward she would never be sure exactly what had caused in her a swoon so instantaneous that it went altogether unnoticed by her partner. Was it the feel of the luxurious gabardine that exquisitely blanketed his back; or the aroma of his cologne mixed with a uniquely natural scent which evoked childhood memories of her father snatching her up and holding her close? Or was it the delicious restraint of his embrace; or that truly lovely smile of complicity and confidence he presented her in the one moment when she dared to meet his gaze; or the strength of his presence as he swept her up; or the power of his body to direct hers as they moved in circles upon circles to the brilliant strains of the music that she could not resist? As if completely subdued to his will, she found, to her great surprise, she was a captive to the intricate, dangerous patterns of the dance.

Wake up, Emma Davenant! This cannot be you, dancing at Carleton House; and Beau Leicester is not your partner, nor is Simon here, watching like a falcon from the sidelines, his face dark with envy. Such miracles are not available to difficult girls.

And yet she knew it was true, knew that for the first time she was graceful, perfectly graceful despite her fevered condition and the mad speed of the dance. Faster and faster he whirled her, and still she kept up with him, as if they were flying together. Now the music was building to a crescendo, and only then, as they whirled and whirled and whirled in the ecstasy of the dance, did she sneak a glance around his shoulder to see if Simon was still watching. Indeed he was; the whole assembled company watched, including the other waltzers, most of whom had retired to chairs to observe Beau Leicester and his new partner dance as never before.

As the assuredness of Emma's movements became apparent to Marcus, he drew back his head only far enough to smile and exclaim, "Emma, you are a treasure! A treasure!"

Inspired by the whiskey and the music to a delirious self-confidence of which she never would have believed herself capable, Emma fluttered her lashes as she observed, "And you, too, are a treasure, Marcus. Why hasn't some lovely gentlewoman snatched you up?"

Even as she was swept on by the dance, Emma could feel her soaring spirits plummet. For her query had, almost imperceptibly but no less surely, dimmed the dazzling gaiety in Marcus's glance.

As he began to speak, a look of something very like regret played briefly upon his handsome features. "Ah, Lady Emma," he smiled, displaying a casual joviality that belied his unease, "my fiancée has called me many things, but never, I daresay, a treasure."

70

"And where have you hidden her, your fiancée?" Emma demanded with a piquant charm meant to disguise her disappointment that all dreams, like dances, must end.

It seemed to Emma that Marcus paled slightly beneath the courtly smile. "She's not in England at the moment," he tossed back. "Traveling abroad."

"Is she English? Might I know her?" she inquired politely.

"She has spent some time in England," he replied quite smoothly, dipping her low and whirling her even faster. "But we met on the Continent."

"Oh," his partner said lightly, reminding herself that, after all, the private lives of servants were their own affair. "And have you set a date for the wedding?"

Again a suave smile graced his words. "Only in the most general fashion. Have no fear, Lady Emma, my engagement shall have no effect on our . . . arrangement."

"I am so glad to hear that, Lord Leicester," she responded, surprised herself at the irritation that rang through the phrase.

Now he was twirling her so fast that she once more sustained a momentary swoon; and then, the music stopped, and the dance ended.

"And what a lucky lady she is, your fiancée," she tossed back at him as he walked off the floor and she moved toward Simon, whose entire body visibly trembled, whether in absolute adoration or complete astonishment she knew not.

71

Chapter IX

ALTHOUGH THE HOUR had grown late, Carleton House sparkled ever more brightly. Emma observed that the couples who now surrounded them were even more dazzling than those amongst whom she and Marcus had waltzed earlier. The candles glowed with a greater radiance, the music sang more rapturously, and they seemed to have been dancing forever; so long that she had forgotten whatever it was that had upset her. She was so happy. She must after all be dreaming, to be so perfectly contented, as on and on they waltzed.

Suddenly, strangely, through the lush mist of the music a voice called, "Marcus!" Emma knew he must have distinctly heard the call, but he in no way acknowledged it.

Then again the woman's voice, somehow familiar, chimed, "Marcus! Marcus! You promised! You promised!" And it was at that moment that Emma broke from his arms, whirled around toward the terrace, and saw, silhouetted in the doorway, the beckoning, beautiful, hideous form of Florissa de Coucy, who now moved into the room toward the frozen form of Marcus, whose look of horror was turning into a leer of sensual pleasure. . . .

"Madame, madame!" Suddenly Emma shot up through her nightmarish despair, and blessedly found herself in the middle of her own bed, with the sunlight of Belgrave Square pouring in through her own windows, and her own Gillings urgently calling her name.

"Yes, Gillings, whatever is the—*ouch*!" The slight movement of raising her head from the pillow had, to Emma's great surprise, provoked the onset of a cruel megrim. And, following on the heels of that ache, came a thirst worthy of a Bedouin lost on the deserts of Araby. Next the forceful complaint of her sadly neglected stomach reminded her that, having declined to partake of last midnight's repast, she had eaten nothing in almost a day. "Gillings, I have the most awesome pain in the head. And the greatest thirst. And I am starving! Wherever's my breakfast?"

"Madame, there is no time! You must arise. And dress. Lord Leicester has only just arrived and is presently ascending our very steps with the intention of entering your bedchamber!"

The pleasure which the message induced in her was reproved by the nagging finger of disappointment. She recalled her tutor's commitment, and the dreadful nightmare. Instinctively she bristled, "Well, Gillings, turn right around, march to the steps, and stop him!"

"Stop him, mum?" So aghast was the tone that one would have thought that, rather than simply having him halted, Emma had suggested that Marcus be put to the sword.

"Yes, Gillings," Emma muttered impatiently. "Stop him before it's too—"

"Good morning, Lady Emma!" And into the bedchamber strode a suave and smiling Marcus. That Emma chose not to respond to his greeting seemed not in the least to fluster the affianced cupid. Once Gillings had made a strangely girlish little curtsy and retired, he crossed to Emma and gently took the hand which was not occupied in drawing the bedclothes up to her neck.

Her hand in his brought back too vividly the memories of last night's dance and caused Emma to reply, rather too airily, "Lord Leicester! I assumed you would still be waltzing!"

Dropping her hand with delicacy, he proceeded to pull a chair up to the bedside and continued to address politely the figure sinking beneath the bedclothes. "Oh, no," he replied unflappably. "I took my leave only moments after you and Lord Jason."

"Oh, really; I should have thought the ladies would have ambushed you by the end of the evening and carried you off, a captive, to some obscure retreat." And she smiled archly.

The possible glint of distress in his eyes could, of course, have been the product of Emma's imagination. "No," he responded as brightly as ever, "I fought my way out." At that she managed the meanest of small and mirthless chuckles.

Seemingly oblivious, Marcus pursued the conversation as casually as if they were meeting of an afternoon in Rotten Row. "And how are you feeling this . . . this afternoon?" he concluded.

"This *afternoon*?" Emma was truly shocked. "Oh, Lord, what time is it?"

He paused, seeming unwilling to hazard a mere estimate. Drawing an elegant thin gold chronometer from his heather tweed waistcoat pocket, he clicked it open and scrutinized it before returning it to its resting place.

"Going on one," Marcus allowed, then continued, "and you're going to be up and about before the clock strikes two, for, unless I miss my guess, your drawing room will be overflowing with suitors by half past that hour."

Mystified as she was by the great Beau's prognostication, she warily inquired, "Suitors? In my drawing room?"

"Ah, yes, Lady Emma; your debut, you know, was a triumph!" Could it have been something akin to pride—or yearning—that stirred in the gray-blue depths of his eyes as he proceeded? "And if you were to ask me to name some of the beaux soon to crowd your saloon, I would mention the young Earl of Coventry, that eminent widower, the Marquis of Somerset, the twin Dukes of Devonshire, Harry Percy from up North, Anthony Chase, and, last, but far from least, Lord Jason."

Fascinated in spite of herself, Emma emerged rather more boldly from under the blankets and demanded, "A triumph? How do you know?"

"After you and Lord Jason had so hastily retreated, I remained at the affair only long enough to be cornered by those aforementioned gentlemen, among many others, hungry to know of the lovely and spirited lady on my arm." And he could not resist a broader smile.

Emma, however, refused to admit a victory. "Well, we'll just have to see," she said, noncommittal. Then, suddenly realizing that two o'clock would arrive all too quickly, she began to rise from the bed; but she was struck with a fresh attack of megrim and she sank back, legs dangling over the side of the bed, head in her hands.

At once he was at her side, grasping her shoulders and lifting her onto the bed, where he propped her up against the pillows. "Close your eyes," he ordered her quite sweetly. "Just rest until the dizziness is past."

As she obeyed him, she could not help but inquire, "How did you know I was dizzy?" Perhaps he had drugged her! Perhaps he drugged all unsuspecting females. Just then, his gentle voice interrupted the dangerous progress of her thoughts.

"Alas, I know all too well the sickness produced by— and I reproach myself for this—by the whiskey."

"By the whiskey? What do you mean by the whiskey?" Was he now indeed confessing he had drugged her? But, hold, for he continued.

"I attempted to stop you, Lady Emma, you will recall. Nevertheless I certainly accept full blame for this most unfortunate occurrence. You see . . ."

And all at once it struck her, with a moral anguish far surpassing the pain of the megrim: she had been intoxicated. So intoxicated that she had only the most abstract memories of the evening. And what of the things she had done and forgotten? What of the true intensity of the actions she could only vaguely recall? Was he mocking her? Or trying to assuage her unhappy guilt? Had she, in fact, made a fool of herself? Coldly, with all the dignity she could muster, she managed a dignified response. "I assume I was intoxicated."

His silence was response enough.

"And may I also assume that, under the influence of—" the pause was condemnation "—this *whiskey*, I behaved in an unusual fashion?"

"Ah, yes," he beamed, "most unusual." She knew then that she was surely ruined; but he broke into her despairing thoughts again. "And most, most delightful you were, too. You seemed to be having quite a good time."

"I did?" She was not of a mind to trust him.

As if he were a mesmerist reading her thought, he

countered her cynicism. ''You need not take my word for it. Wait until half past two and see for yourself.''

And she was forced, in all reason, to accept his point, although it by no means cleared him of the charges of villainy.

''However,'' he continued, ''unless you wish to receive a squad of love-crazed suitors in your bedchamber, we must be up and about.''

Struck by the notion that what she had always wanted might now lie within her grasp, Emma once more attempted to rise until once more her head and stomach revolted against the idea. ''Oooh.'' She had no recourse but to throw herself on his mercy. ''But what shall I do for my poor head? It aches so awfully. And I am starved! And thirsty! And dizzy! And sallow, I'll wager. And I suppose my eyes are red and swollen!''

''Now, now.'' With a nanny's compassion, he leaned forward to pat the hand that had relaxed its hold on the coverlet. ''You mustn't fret. Anticipating your complaint, I've already set about arranging the remedy. Any moment now, Miss Gillings will—'' As usual his words seemed to invoke the image he described, for Miss Gillings just then appeared at the door bearing a large silver tray whose mysterious contents were hidden under a snowy damask cloth. ''Ah, Miss Gillings, I'll take that,'' and the physician in spite of himself promptly relieved the good lady of her burden, which he proceeded to set down on a lacquered bedside table.

Craning her neck for a preview of the bounteous prescription, Emma felt the ache return with a vengeance. ''Gillings, bring the laudanum,'' she commanded, but the servant seemed rooted to the spot in which she stood. ''Gillings! The laudanum! At once!''

But Gillings's only response was to cast a desperate

77

glance in Marcus's direction. "Begging your pardon, ma'am," the obviously upset lady began, "but . . ."

"I am sorry, Lady Emma, I have ordered Gillings to give you no laudanum!"

And all at once Emma flew into a fury. "What do you mean, *you* have ordered Gillings? You forget, Lord Leicester, that this is my house. Gillings! At once!"

The torment of conflict was evident in the face of the good lady, but still she did not move, and Emma's voice rose shrilly. "Gillings!"

The agony of the lady was blessedly relieved by Marcus's further unruffled explanation. "Yes, Lady Emma, it is indeed your house. As it is your life. And if you intend to greet your suitors in a drug-induced stupor, I will heartily convey the bottle to you myself. I cannot believe that effect is truly the one you desire."

"Perhaps not," she responded, her fire dampened. Then, suspiciously, she demanded, "And what, instead, would you suggest?"

"Ah," he proclaimed, slowly raising the cloth on the tray to reveal an alchemist's array of goblets and pitchers of unknown substances. "Now you will try my own version of laudanum," and he indicated a large goblet of bright red liquid, a tall slim bottle containing a crystalline fluid, numerous small bottles and jars, and a large bowl of small, shining cubes. "Trust me, this remedy has never, in my experience, failed to ameliorate a condition such as yours. You must be curious as to the identity of these many elements."

Still incensed by his household *coup d'état*, she refused to grant him the pleasure of her curiosity; nevertheless she was relieved that he would freely offer the information. "Since it is clearly intended for my consumption, I would appreciate a catalog of the possible dangers of this potion," she replied with all the haughtiness she could summon up.

"Be assured, Lady Emma." He had crossed behind the table and was now rubbing his hands together as he surveyed the tray's contents, clearly anticipating the preparation of the brew. "The dangers are far from great. Never would I attempt to poison you, for then I should be cut off from not only the satisfaction of my employment, but from my source of income as well." At this he grinned, to Emma's mind rather too wickedly.

Refusing to admit to any emotion whatsoever, Emma parried idly. "A thousand thanks, Lord Leicester, for now I do feel enormously reassured."

"Your humble servant, ma'am," he uttered with what might have been a hint of sarcasm. "Now." He commenced his alchemy by raising high the red elixir. "First, we begin with this fearful concoction. Although it appears terribly threatening, it's actually quite tasteful. Can't hazard even a guess as to what it is, I'll wager." Without waiting for her reply, he speedily informed her. "This substance is the juice of a small cylindrical fruit indigenous to the Americas which is actually consumed as a legume. So strange is the appearance and taste that the natives first thought it was poisoned, and feared it, then considered it magical, and termed it a love apple. Now, it is referred to as the *tomato* from the American native term *tomatl*. Several years ago a friend from New York brought me some of the verdurous plants, which my man has managed to nurture quite successfully all year round in my greenhouse garden. Thus, I was able to bring enough of the fruits for this restorative to be extracted.

"Next," putting down the goblet and indicating the tall bottle, "here's a little something I learned of from a captured French officer in the Peninsula. Quite a fine fella he was, too. Had seen action in the Russian campaign, where he'd

79

first enjoyed the benefits of this excellent potion.'' As if she had inquired, he explained, "Made from potatoes, it is. And only in the Russias. Still my vintner is somehow able to keep me in adequate supply. Called *vodka*."

"Vodka," Emma murmured idly as Marcus now produced a magnificently large, golden lemon (undoubtedly grown in his own miraculous greenhouse), which he proceeded to cut into quarters with a small silver knife.

"And now we begin," he laughed lightly, extracting a frosty goblet from the bowl of what appeared to be cubes of ice. Her curiosity must have been manifest. As if reading her thoughts again, he declared, "Yes, the cubes are ice, and the glass is frosted to just the proper point of refreshment. Actually it was first in America that I heard tell of a device, invented by an American who, funnily enough, had emigrated to England. He had designed a box which was said to maintain a freezing temperature within, no matter what the climate or season. I immediately commenced correspondence with the inventive gentleman, one Mr. Perkin, and now my kitchen staff can keep food cool and fresh and make ice all year round, thanks to Mr. Perkin's icebox."

Although Emma was moved to question the veracity of his claim, she chose instead not to give Marcus the satisfaction of a response. He did not seem to mind her silence as he busied himself with his preparations.

"And now we take this glass and add just this much of the vodka.

"Next, a dash of condiment from the Caribes—made from the exotic tamarind fruit, molasses, sugar, very tasty in small amounts. Next, a hearty dollop of the gratings of a root called the horseradish; now the juice of this most piquant lemon. And we stir." He interrupted his alchemy briefly to look up with a jolly smile, which was most distinctly not met with like response. Undeterred he persevered, "At this precise moment, we add the juice of the tomato, but not to the brim, for we must keep in mind that, after a second stirring, thus! we will add the ice cubes!" And he triumphantly raised a small pair of exquisite silver tongs and proceeded to transfer three of the glittering packets of water into the frosted goblet. "One final stir, and, *voilà*! Madame, your remedy." With great panache he presented the devilish brew to a still skeptical Emma, who, rather than raising it to her lips, chose instead to study the glass.

"Come now, Lady Emma, be brave and try it! Believe me, you will find the beverage to be astonishingly refreshing . . . if I do say so, myself . . ."

But she was not so easily to be conquered. "But, Lord Leicester, will you not join me?"

"I think not, madame, for I am not suffering from your condition."

"But, surely, even you, sir, would welcome a refreshment. Would you not?" And it presented itself quite clearly to Marcus that she would not drink unless he drank first. "Of course, madame, I would be more than glad to join you," and he returned to the table where, under Emma's hawklike observation, he prepared a second drink. Then he seated himself, raising his glass in her direction, and met her appraising gaze with a dazzling smile and a brief toast, "Here's looking at you, madame!" And they both drank deeply.

To Emma's astonishment, the concoction was more than refreshing. It was delicious. The tart yet sweet juice of the tomato, enlivened by the icy white heat of the vodka, rippled down her throat concluding in a spicy aftertaste which made her crave more of the stately iciness of the vodka. Even she could not deprive Marcus of the acknowledgment of his achievement. "Umm," she announced judiciously. "Quite tasty," and she punctuated the compliment with a second long draught.

"A word of warning, Lady Emma. You must sip this beverage. An overabundance will provoke in you the return of the very state you seek to banish."

The warning was sufficient to slow her pace, as was the entry of the cook bearing yet another tray. "Your breakfast, madame," she announced, bearing her treasure solemnly to the bedside and arranging the tray on Emma's lap.

Soon the covers of the dishes were removed, and still another surprise awaited her. "And what is this aromatic concoction, Lord Leicester?"

"An invention of my man, who has served as my cook since our years in the service. I accuse him of having picked it up from a Frenchie, but he denies it. He starts with a sort of muffin of his own devising. Invented it on campaign, since it does not need to rise and keeps for quite a long time. Soon the whole British fleet was eating them, then the other friendly fleets. Hence he calls it an 'English' muffin. Adorning the muffin, a slice of ham, topped by a poached egg, which is, in turn, crowned with a sauce we learned of in the Netherlands, miraculous in its succulence— and a damned nuisance to do well . . . I see Cook has succeeded brilliantly, however. I urge you to try it, madame, it will be delicious."

And of course it was, all creamy and salty and infinitely soothing, its heady richness relieved perfectly by an occasional sip of the piquant beverage. Even now, Marcus's prediction as to the brew's effects were borne out, for Emma found her headache disappearing, and both her spirits and confidence rising.

"Lady Emma, you're looking considerably improved already."

She was prepared to reward him with the barest possible

smile, when a knock on the door was followed by the entry of Harsant, who announced, "Madame, three gentlemen have stopped by to call on you, and having been told you are not risen, insist that they will return at two, quarter past two, and half past two, respectively."

"Is Lord Jason among them?" Emma asked boldly.

"Ah yes, madame, Lord Jason is the two o'clock. The quarter past two is Sir Anthony Chase, and the Marquis of Somerset arrives at half past the hour. I would like to take the liberty to remind madame that the clock is already well past the hour of one."

"Ah yes, I must hurry," murmured Emma, reluctantly pushing aside her breakfast. When she looked up again, she found Marcus gazing at her with laughter in his eyes, as he half whispered words meant for her ears only. "The hunt commences, madame. Tally-ho!"

Chapter X

MARCUS, HAVING DELIVERED his recovered charge into the good hands of Gillings and Lucy to be dressed, was free to repair to the burgundy saloon in order to appear to the *ton* the earliest, and therefore the most ardent, of all Lady Emma's swains.

Counting on at least a half hour of solitude, he had brought with him a German volume titled *Die Wahlverwandtschaften*; it was a personal gift from its author, Johann von Goethe, with whom Marcus had recently shared hours of priceless conversation at the doctor's home in Weimar. The novel he found more pleasurable even than the master's description of it, and it was to his great regret as well as surprise that his delight was interrupted after a few moments by the premature arrival of Lord Jason.

One needed only to glance at the smile frozen on the poet's face to appreciate his awful disappointment at having been preceded hence. "Lord Leicester," he intoned, the rippling civility of his remarks threatened by an undertow of resentment, "how enter*taining* to find you here so une*xpec*tedly."

"And vice versa," Marcus fairly chirped, closing his book preparatory to replacing it in his pocket.

Having stalked to a brocade chair and rigidly seated himself, the poet now inquired, "And what would the volume be, Lord Leicester?"

As he offered the book for Simon's perusal, he answered, "The great novel of Dr. Goethe . . . in English, it would be called something like *Elective Affinities*."

"Oh, really," Simon icily retorted, before looking down at the leather-bound volume he now grasped. Once he did, however, his face clouded over.

"Do you read German, Lord Jason?" Marcus asked with apparent innocence.

"Actually, no." The poet thrust the book back at Marcus. "It seems to me that in this modern age there is no need to seek beyond one's mother tongue or one's own epoch to find greatness."

How noble, mused Marcus, or how foppish, to measure beauty and greatness only by one's own experience. Simon's sense of history, the Beau decided, must be even more deficient than his sense of wit.

In the uneasy silence that followed, Marcus strained his intellect to discover just what it was about the brattish boy that Emma so adored. Clearly the poet's lack of manners could be traced directly to his general disregard for tradition. But that so demanding a woman as Emma should find that rudeness flattering defied Marcus's understanding. Once again he set about cataloging the poet's dubious qualities: the great sullenness, comprised of hostile silence interspersed with unwilling efforts at conversation, the lack of generosity, the childish self-absorption that always threatened a tantrum, the unabashed embracing of personal opportunity at others' expense. Yet these flaws evidently produced a romantic portrait invisible to Marcus. *Romantic!* Perhaps that word was the key! It was the unpredictability of passions that so ensorcelled her. Passions!

For Jason, and most probably for Emma, the ordering of emotions amounted to the betrayal of one's own nature. To them, love was chaos and chaos love, and law was oppression. For Emma, Jason's spoiled erratic behavior was obviously exciting. And if that were the case, did it mean that she found Marcus dull, or as Admiral Davenant had suggested, silly? Him—silly! They were the silly geese, both of 'em!

For no apparent reason Jason's passionate tossing of his blond curls provoked in Marcus the origin of a feeling too odd to be assigned the label of envy. It was a curious emotion, one well worth defining, and he was diverted from this self-examination only by the poet's sunny query, "Ah! And where in the world is *our* dear Emma?"

Although he bristled inwardly at the employment of that demeaning pronoun, Marcus restrained himself from any overt breach of good form. "Can't really say. Been waiting longer than you have, old boy."

Suddenly narrowing his eyes in an expression of great shrewdness, Simon defiantly announced, "I was here earlier, you know. I was, in fact, the first to call this morning."

"Let us hope Lady Emma has been informed of that fact," Marcus responded graciously, "for I hear we two shall not be the only callers of the afternoon."

Simon chose not to comment upon his rival's *coup.* Instead he returned to the more pressing subject at hand. "How long *have* you been waiting?" he inquired peevishly.

"Oh," Marcus let his eyes drift skyward in a look of tolerant exasperation, "almost an hour."

"Almost an hour?" Simon was clearly distressed. "With no word from upstairs."

"Not so far," Marcus allowed and punctuated the dispatch with an energetic flick of his cigarette's ashes into the fireplace.

As if on cue, another substantial presence added itself to the uneasy company. Simon had noted the new arrival first, provoking in him great dismay, as witnessed by his hissing, "Oh, Lord! It's Barnaby!"

The fearful adversary now advanced from the door to the center of the room, where he assumed a stance of malevolent grandeur, confronting the rivals with a glance that both condemned and dismissed them.

"Barnaby. Yes. We've met." Marcus offered up this amiable opening, which the redoubtable Barnaby chose to ignore. Fearlessly the Beau shifted his gaze 'til his blue-gray eyes locked with the arrival's glowing ember ones. "So you're called Barnaby, eh?" Marcus inquired quite cheerfully to the great alp of a cat over whom he had exited this very room only the day before.

In response the presence remained immobile as a stone, his enigmatic gaze still intent upon Marcus's as it had been the afternoon the monstrous feline had tripped him.

"That . . . *thing*," Simon began venomously, "is the great love of Emma's life. She feeds him only on chickens' livers with sherry and shallots and cream. That beast. Terrorizes every dog, cat, and serving maid in the neighborhood, he does, during his . . . periodic sojourns . . . away. I'd like to strangle him with that lovely blue ribbon she ties around his neck!"

During this denunciation, the great cat had slowly, with an assassin's assuredness, begun to flick his short, stocky cannon of a tail. Momentarily shifting his eyes, he bestowed on the poet a killing glance, then returned to Marcus, who seized the occasion to employ his great gift for pacifying difficult women and animals. "Well, Barnaby," he commenced, deciding to treat the housecat to a most amusing game, "what kind of bird makes this sound?" And, miraculously, he reproduced the warble of a bluebird.

At first Barnaby's response was almost inaudible. Then it grew in volume, and Marcus, delighted, knew he had won. "Am I mistaken, or is that a purr I hear issuing from the beast?"

"A purr?" Simon answered contemptuously. "A purr? More like a growl, I'd say. Watch when it gets louder. That's when he'll leap at you."

And, sure enough, the sound increased in amplitude. Still Barnaby stared unblinking at the Beau, his amber eyes glowing in open challenge, his tail beating its deadly tattoo.

"Barnaby," Marcus announced respectfully, "I feel I've misjudged you. Though some may see you as . . . overbearing . . . I find you rather elegant. No, not elegant; perhaps handsome is the word." The animal remained poised for the attack. "No—that's still not quite right— not handsome so much as *dignified*."

Simon was elated by the prospect of witnessing a martyr's death at the claws of a lion. And yet he had to admire the Beau's courage for he could feel his own heart pound as Barnaby, gaze still leveled at Marcus, actually began to rise. Slowly he unsheathed his powerful claws . . .

Although Simon's eyes had clamped themselves shut for only a moment, he was surprised to hear no scream. Slowly allowing the room to slip back into view, he observed the cat with his front paws extended and his claws digging not into Marcus, but rather into the deep and priceless Oriental carpet. After a few moments of luxurious stretching, Barnaby turned and strolled magnificently toward a graceful little gold chair. Once attaining his destination, he leaped heavily upon the cushion, curled his great bulk into a good-sized bundle, and proceeded instantly to snooze.

Marcus, surprised to feel a slight weakness in his knees, allowed himself a moment of relief and a cigarette.

During the succeeding resumption of their silent vigil, Marcus seized the opportunity to set into motion his next gambit. "I say, Simon," he allowed with just the correct admixture of the *faux* friend and the beggar. "You wouldn't happen to have five quid on you, would you? I . . . I'm . . . a bit down in the pocket right now and I have to pay off a gambling debt."

He had struck home! Simon's eyes instantly lit up with malicious glee. Before the sun went down, news of Lord Leicester's penury would be sweeping the town, and with it, confirmation that the Beau had fallen quite in love with Emma's fortune. Once the venal nature of his intentions was known, Emma's prospective husbands might be flushed out faster, prompted by the fear that Leicester might grab her off any moment.

That Lord Jason was the perfect messenger for such tidings was evidenced by the warmth and *bonhomie* with which he cheerfully bubbled, "Glad to, old man, any time," and reached into his pocket. But the ill-disguised pain with which he extracted the bills suddenly told Marcus that the poet's rekindled ardor was inspired by financial desperation. The fop himself was in it for the fortune! And that meant that the selfish wretch might throw Emma over again should a larger fortune present itself. As Marcus fervently renewed his vow to find an honest lover for Emma, the door opened and the blushing object of his thoughts tripped daintily into the room perfectly per his instructions.

Ignoring two of the company, she delightedly discovered the third and cried, "Barnaby, dear! You're back from your travels!" At which the infernal creature roused himself, leaped nimbly off the chair, and made straight for his mistress's embrace.

The arrival of the hour of four came none to soon for the exhausted company in the burgundy saloon. Only moments after Emma's stylish entrance, the other suitors had arrived, all in a bunch, despite Harsant's previous efforts to stagger their visits. And once there, *en masse*, none would admit defeat by retiring first from the lists of love; hence they remained, all of them, battling one another for Emma's attention with a ferocity that astonished her.

The young Earl of Coventry, fatally smitten, poor victim of puppy love, persisted in hurling himself onto his knees before her. The red-haired, hot-tempered Harry Percy repeatedly attempted to dislodge the lecherous Anthony Chase from the choice seat next to milady on the settee, where he was desperately clutching for her hand. That prize, however, had already been secured by the palsied claw of the Marquis of Somerset, which antique gentleman having bowed low, was now attempting to disguise as humble reverence the great time it took him to straighten up again. Meanwhile the twin Dukes of Devonshire were stationed at either end of the sofa glaring at one another, unable to decide whether, in this theater of war, they were allies or mortal enemies. Milady herself was seated with consummate grace, her lap overflowing with the unmoving but ardent Barnaby, now purring with an almost frightening intensity. And Lord Jason, fancying himself, as earliest claimant, the lady's sole, true, and rightful suitor, had secured a splendidly central situation from which he refused to move: he smiled continually down upon Emma from behind the settee, his arms spread out to encompass the entire back of the couch, as if in symbolic possession of the lady who occupied it.

Only Marcus, of all the warriors gathered for this great engagement, kept his distance from the demure objective. From his vantage point near the fire, he was enjoying the fact that no one in the romantic melee was paying the slightest attention to him. Smoking, without noticing, one cigarette after another, he was most powerfully interested in his pupil's flawless performance. She was every inch her father's daughter, and the valor of her determination gratified his partisan expectation. With the purposeful grace of a true thoroughbred, she had maneuvered through the press of suitors, managing to engage one with a smile, another with a whispered word, flattering all while neglecting none. Her spirit excited and pleased him, as he silently cheered her on.

Simon, still smiling benignly upon the lady of his affections, was, nonetheless, internally in turmoil. Fevered for Emma's attention, as well as her fortune, he was all too aware that both commodities might be perilously close to forfeiture, through no fault of his own. His last remaining chance was to proceed far more rapidly than his previous plans had prescribed. Damn that Leicester! So sure of himself that he need not even bother to play the courting game. There he sailed, steering out of harm's way, his face a mask of utter indifference! That he, too, was after Emma's money was no longer in doubt. Anthony Chase, Harry Percy, and the twin Dukes had already, rest assured, been informed of Leicester's bankruptcy, and were champing at the bit to be the first at Watier's with the grievous news. How careless of Leicester to reveal his secret to his foremost rival! How great must be his need! Simon would be a fool not to press the advantage. Frankly, however, the zeal of the powerful and well-heeled beaux who crowded the saloon filled the poet with greater concern. They, whose legacies were well intact, seemed to be suing for Emma's affection with a frenzy equal to his own. And with some reason: for it had to be admitted that, during his absence, the awkward, sharp-tongued slip of a girl had become quite a lovely lady. Bad piece o' luck, her growing desirable and proud just when he needed her abject. Still he could not allow the competition to frighten him off. His tailor had been the first to call upon his return, and it was not to welcome him home. And his vintner had only yesterday delivered a copy of an old but frightening tally, accompanied by a threatening note. And there was worse—far worse—to come. Clearly he no longer had a choice. He *must* wed Emma, and there was an end to it.

Emma, eyes dancing with triumph, glanced provocatively up at Simon, and then, as she lowered her gaze back down toward the kneeling Earl of Coventry, managed to steal a look at the languid figure of Marcus, lounging, in a posture of supreme disinterest, near the fireplace. That he was the only man in the room not paying her intimate attention provoked her to another unexpected rage. Even Simon, the usually chill and sullen Simon, was trying his best to wrest her attention from the other beaux. But not Marcus. Oh no, never the worldly wise and promised Beau, to whom a job of work was merely a job of work. As the clock struck four, Emma gathered up Barnaby in her arms, rose (with a darling little yawn), and prepared her exit, graciously accepting a floral showering of compliments and invitations. But in her heart the insult of Leicester's indifference still smoldered; and it was then she decided to give the teacher a lesson he would be hard put to forget.

Chapter XI

EMMA'S SPIRITS HELD high and steady for the following few weeks. Only at odd moments, in the middle of the tempest which had caught her up, a certain despair overtook her. In novels one's life could become fabulous whilst one languished abed, in one's spectacles, petting one's cat, drinking one's chocolate, and reading one's book. In real life, however, at least in real life à la Leicester, one all too frequently wondered if anything or any man, even Simon, was worth the risk, the running, the rehearsal, and the nightmarish upheaval which had become her existence. Even her house could no longer be called her own. Certainly, had she been led in blindfolded, and then unmasked, she would not have guessed in whose domicile she stood.

Leicester, with Harsant's manly aid, had miraculously assembled an elite army of painters, upholsterers, furniture makers, rug merchants, drapiers, chandlers, mirror men, art purveyors, and general refinishers, all of whom seemed willing to work through the night and even on Sundays. Inexhaustibly, like demonic elves, they set about reducing everything familiar to the newest states of strangeness. Without so much as the soliciting of her opinion, Emma's familiar household haunts had been utterly transformed, just as her old dressing gown, now permanently retired to a place of honor in the back of the wardrobe, had been replaced by a chic creation of light peach silk, subtly decorated with the finest of brown satin ribbons.

In fact, the lush peach color of this dressing gown, chosen personally by Marcus Leicester to adorn the mistress of the house, was owned so flattering to that lady, so perfectly, subtly suited to her own sweet coloring, that it was pronounced Lady Emma's own hue.

Hence the deep blues of her boudoir had been effaced in favor of that color, which the wizards of decor pronounced "péche," and to which Marcus referred as "peach," but which Anne Gillings, Emma's last remaining ally in the preservation of the familiar, succinctly labeled "pink."

Whilst the boudoir was under seige, Emma was banished to the gold-and-white radiance of the hateful chamber that had so lately been designed and occupied by the horrible Florissa. Stalking angrily up and down in front of an overabundance of gold-framed mirrors, Emma felt as lonely, as frightened, as if she had been held prisoner in a dungeon in the Bastille. Even Barnaby only grudgingly consented to keep her company in the enormous, grotesque chamber, and, upon entering, gave forth a small but serious growl before leaping onto the brocade bedspread and languidly, purringly, ripping a section of it to shreds.

Consenting once or twice to quit the boudoir for a tour of the house, Emma was most startled by the rapidity with which the burgundy saloon was subdued to an antique wheat; whilst the drawing room was scarcely recognizable as the pastel green-and-marigold confection now being prepared. Halls brightened and bloomed as if by themselves, and the removal of the heavy window hangings invited the spring light to come dancing in upon the heads of the wonder workers.

At the commencement of this Herculean undertaking, Marcus had informed Emma that for the next few weeks, she would be on holiday from all suitors, including Simon. But Harsant's transmittal of this information did precious little good; for still they pressed, and paced restlessly on the front doorstep, eager to present their cards. At last Harsant was ordered to commend to them Lady Emma's best wishes, and announce that she had gone from London for the next few weeks and would happily receive them upon her return.

"But what shall I tell Simon?" she had demanded of her tutor when he revealed this duplicitous piece of strategy to her.

"Tell him nothing, Lady Emma," Marcus answered with extraordinary assurance. They were sitting in the kitchen; the dining room was still in a shambles, the kitchen was the only quarter of the topsy-turvy house in which a civilized conversation might still be held. And so it was here that Emma found herself for the very first time. Cook, of course, was shocked that the mistress and her magnificent instructor would stoop to cocoa with the servants; but, after being sweetly cajoled by the conveniently libertarian Marcus, she consented to a temporary suspension of custom and actually fed them cookies still hot from the oven.

"How can I tell him nothing?" Emma persevered. "Simon will think I have forsaken him." And she assumed the most downcast of expressions.

Cook, however, ostensibly occupied with the quenelles

which would later be enjoyed by the hoi polloi on this selfsame kitchen table, could not resist breaking in. "Oh, no, madame. Begging your pardon, but Lord Leicester is quite correct, if I take his meaning. A lady must play, a bit, at being unobtainable; it is an excellent tactic for securing a lover's affections."

Briefly wondering once more about the source of Cook's profound knowledge of the intricacies of the *ton*, Emma shook her head. "I don't want to do that. I don't want to be dishonest or cruel."

"Lady Emma," Marcus advised her sternly, "I think you fear your cruelty less than you fear his loss of interest. And I promise you, your fears are groundless. For what you shall do is send him a message in which you declare your urgent need for a bit of country air and promise to contact him the instant you are back in town. His assumption that you have gone to some pastoral hideaway in my company can only make his pursuit more zealous. Trust me, Lady Emma," he implored, as Cook seconded, "Trust him, mum," without looking up from her quenelles.

It was only after the note had been delivered, and news of Lady Emma's mysterious departure from London in the probable company of the Beau Leicester circulated, that the exhausting wardrobe work began. At great expense, partially to insure the secrecy of the project as well as its speed, Marcus had gathered the finest and most trustworthy company of milliners, dressmakers, glove makers, shoe purveyors, furriers, ribbon merchants, jewelers, and other professional arbiters of fashion. In droves they came, measuring her, fitting her, pricking her with pins and making her feet fall asleep from standing so long in the same position. They consulted with Marcus and with each other in her presence as if she had been invisible, referring to her as "she," and talking with shocking frankness about the liabilities—and occasionally the embarrassing assets—of her form and style.

Her few most treasured garments, including the ancient dressing gown she was no longer allowed to wear, had accompanied her into the exile of Florissa's room, whilst the greater part of the collection remained in the wardrobe in her boudoir. Or so she thought until, upon inquiring as to the whereabouts of her red silk frock with the blue and yellow dewdrops, she was informed by Marcus that it had been discarded.

"Then what about the purple velvet with the red fox at the neckline? I *loved* that dress!" His silence told her that she was after all being held prisoner in her own house, with hardly a stitch of clothing in which she might make her escape.

"Then may I see the progress of the boudoir, Lord Leicester?" she begged one desperate morning over the fresh croissants in whose preparation Marcus had instructed Cook.

"No, Lady Emma, best put that off until it is all done, and your new wardrobe is in your cupboards waiting for you. It'll only be a matter of days."

And the time did pass swiftly, or so it seemed, due largely, she had to admit, to the strangely calming presence of Marcus in the midst of this frenzy that was, yet, of his own devising.

"Let me warn you, Lady Emma, that this upheaval will seem like a gentle spring mist compared to the tempestuous *ton* life into which you will be swept in the weeks to come." Marcus offered her some of Cook's most succulent apricot jam and smiled rather gently. "There will be moments when you will look back upon this solitude with a certain nostalgia." Raising her gaze from her plate to his handsome and gracious countenance, she wondered if he might not be right.

And at last the great day arrived. It was the middle of the morning, yet Emma lolled abed in the white-and-gold chamber, spectacles perched midnose and hair tousled, quite caught up in Mary Shelley's most hypnotizing work of the imagination, *Frankenstein*. At his mistress's side lounged Barnaby, intently working the destruction of one small square of brocade, purring all the while.

So engaged were the pair in their various pursuits that it took two knocks before Emma admitted the caller, her excellent tutor, cutting an exceedingly gallant figure in navy gabardine coat and fawn trousers, his snowy white shirt glowing against the radiance of his paisley cravat.

"Good day, Lady Emma," he announced gaily, and then, "and good day to you too, old boy," he added. The cat shot him a brief glance of resentment at this untoward familiarity, but wisely sensing that restraint was in order, shifted his attention quickly back to the brocade battle-ground beneath his claws.

"Lady Emma." Marcus crossed to the huge window nearest him, pulled back the draperies, and opened the window to admit a fresh and eager breeze. "I urge you to put down your book and accompany me to your new boudoir!"

"Oh, you mean it's ready!" She was up in a flash, although Barnaby lingered, loath to participate in so unbecomingly feverish an event. "I'll be ready as soon as I dress."

"Oh, do not bother to change out of your dressing gown, for a hundred new frocks await you only steps away. And do not discard your spectacles before the viewing!"

She paused a moment, catching her breath in preparation for the great event, then smiled at him. "Now," she said firmly.

And he walked to her, offered her his arm, and prepared to escort her in style to face her destiny.

As the pair approached the freshly finished door, all gleaming cherry wood and brass, they were greeted by Harsant, standing stiff and unsmiling, the perfect attendant for a visit of state.

One merry glance from Marcus solicited from Emma the sober response, "All right, I'm ready," and, as Marcus signaled Harsant with a nod, that redoubtable servant commanded the handle of the knob and ushered milady into her chambers.

Deliberately, regally, Emma stepped through the door and into a cloud of morning sunlight. Gone were the dreary darkness of the walls, the heavy window hangings, the somber velvets, the excessive opulence of the curved, gold chairs, the overwhelming stripes of clashing color. The room, which had displayed its magnificence only by moonlight, now glowed with the richness of an early April day, the rose of dawn blending perfectly into the gold of morning. Through the windows, now adorned only with the most gossamer of fabrics, light gamboled and played upon the great bouquets of posies arranged with exquisite, casual elegance among the richly spare lines of the wonderful little chairs upholstered in a darker peach silk and the fine small tables of the lightest cherry wood. The ornate wall sconces of the previous regime had been banished, gone as well were the overwhelming clutter of mirrors and the curios formerly crowding the mantelpiece. But, most astonishing of all, was that the floor had vanished beneath a mist of carpet extending to the four walls. As thick as it was soft, it glowed with a pink-beige pastel radiance that met the peach walls in perfect complement.

"Suits milady's coloring, does it not, Harsant?" From the distance of her private delight, Emma heard Marcus's question and Harsant's polite reply.

"To a tee, milord." And, if she were not mistaken, he allowed himself a half chuckle.

Then they both turned to milady herself, who conquered her rapturous speechlessness long enough to exclaim, "Oh, it's perfection!"

"Shall we proceed into the bedchamber, then, madame?" Harsant suggested, and led them through another door onto another vista of peach and pearl and beige luminescence of velvety carpeting, of smart, spare furniture setting off the satiny peach bed, all reflected endlessly in the grand mirrors which were the walls.

"Oh, Marcus!" she gasped with joy, lowering herself dizzily onto a peach and cherry wood chaise. "It's far too daring."

"No, milady," he retorted jovially, turning toward her. "It is *you*. It is. Only look." He took her hand and raised her to her feet, then turned her toward the mirrored wall. "See, in fact, how the coloring suits yours, how the light encourages the sheen of your hair and the gold plays in the green of your eyes. And see how the style of the room echoes your fresh and open nature, whilst the delicate pastel conveys a frank, yet demure femininity."

Forced to examine herself against a brave new background, Emma had to admit that, once again, the Beau was quite correct. In this room, in this dressing gown, with the light around her and Marcus Leicester beside her, she looked as glamorous as in her most ambitious reveries. Even her spectacles could not detract from the triumphant portrait. Allowing her resolve to slip away, Emma felt rising up in her a sort of gratitude to the man who had made her beautiful even to her own chronically disapproving eyes. And just as the gratitude was giving way to a considerably more dangerous feeling, Marcus interrupted by taking her hand and suggesting, "Shall we go on to the wardrobe?"

As response, she smiled a uniquely radiant smile, then allowed him to escort her across the room, accompanied by the myriad Marcuses and Emmas strolling together in the mirrors around them.

Chapter XII

LADY EMMA'S "RETURN" to London was announced by Marcus the very next day, upon his own reunion with Lord Jason at Wiater's. Casually, and with the graceful conciseness of a gentleman, he allowed as to how he had arrived back from a journey of his own and hightailed it over to Belgrave Square, where he surprised the lady in question just as her carriage was pulling up at the curb.

No amount of wheedling on Simon Herbert's part could coax from the Beau so much as a hint that he had traveled with Emma, even to the other side of Belgravia. In fact, he managed to convey over dinner his irritation with Lady Emma for her refusal to disclose the retreat to which her journey had borne her.

Whilst Anthony Chase, Tommy Somerset, and the twin Dukes of Devon hastily completed their meal and made to rush at once to Belgrave Square, Simon lingered, brooding. Some instinct deep inside his poet's nature warned him that all was not what it seemed; but that same instinct advised him that, were Leicester lying in his teeth, he would not admit the falsehood—in his cups or under torture. God might know what Emma and that dastardly dandy had done, but Simon never would, not, at least, from Marcus, and the frustration of doubt festered in his soul.

The actual sight of Emma, restored to fresh glory in the refurbished town house, did little to allay his fears. How could Simon not perceive that some new happiness had drawn her quiet prettiness into the full sunlight of loveliness? Why was she laughing so merrily when, only weeks before, her damnable sensitivity to his moods would have provoked the onset of a megrim?

"Ah, Simon!" she had practically warbled, turning a little pirouette to indicate to him the wonder of her new surroundings. "I feel like my own woman at last!" But, to Simon, she seemed, for the first time, very much like someone else's.

Granted she was his, and his alone, for the evening, but neither the sultry magic of the ensuing night, nor the myriad charms of Lord Morefield's stunning yacht, could put to rest Simon's fears of displacement.

"Did Leicester accompany you to the country or not, Emma? As your trusted friend, I have a right to know!" Thousands of candles competed with the stars over Simon's head as the yacht wafted languidly up the Thames.

"I shall repeat what I've already told you, Simon," Emma murmured, then inclined her head just so, causing the candlelight to seize up the sparkle of her emeralds.

"No, Emma! That's not good enough," Simon countered angrily. "You must indeed tell me more. Did he, in fact, *accompany* you or *escort* you?"

"Simon Herbert! I don't, for one thing, appreciate the difference. But, even if I did, I would persist in my dismay at your daring to question my virtue! What do you take me for—an actress?'' And Emma made to move away from her companion at the railing.

''Emma! Wait!'' He grasped her silky smooth arm, bare below the champagne velvet of her gown's tiny sleeves. As if on impulse, she paused, then did a perfectly executed *tour*, and studied his ice-blue eyes.

''Simon,'' she urged him gently, ''you know me as well as I know myself. You, better than anyone else, have experienced the great fidelity of my nature.''

As she spoke these soft words, his urge to caress her had increased greatly. As she stood shimmering with stillness, he found himself bending toward her. But, just as he advanced, she moved expertly away, ran across the deck, and paused at the head of the staircase. The strains of waltz music floated up on the still night air.

''Trust me!'' she called. Then, blowing him a kiss, she danced out of his sight and beyond his questions, down the steps toward the waiting waltz.

Chapter XIII

OF COURSE, MARCUS had been correct in his prognostication of Lord Jason's enhanced ardor. Emma's feigned run-off had turned the disaffected poet into a lover of dangerously strong passions. And, as Emma's assurance of his affection increased, her compulsion to take his every sigh as omen, his every mutter as condemnation, quite melted away. She had learned from Marcus, or rather, she had to confess, from his handling of *her*, that one must treat a difficult person as if he or she were not. "Indulge an angry whim, create a brat," she had once heard him admonish the softhearted Gillings. Furious though his words had made her, she had been forced to acknowledge their wisdom.

But it was not only Simon's new attentiveness which was sweetening her nature and stroking her confidence. She had somehow, in the course of her restoration, overcome the fear of being ignored, forgotten, dismissed, or betrayed. It was as if she were indeed a new woman, and a far happier one.

In the course of the busiest week of her life, Marcus had rushed her through route parties, promenades, dinners, suppers, and teas. He had escorted her to Carleton House, to Almack's, to Rotten Row, to the opera, and even to the British Museum to view the "Elgin marbles." He had expertly instructed her in the profitable use of her own attributes: how to flirt with her wit, ensorcel with her eyes, enchant with her petiteness, captivate with the simple smartness of her style. But all this, he informed her, had been only rehearsal for her imminent performance at Mrs. Fitzherbert's. "Lady Emma," Marcus had whispered as they had walked together into the fabulous dining room, "this is your chance to capture the entire town in one fell swoop."

Her quizzical expression had given way to a look of astonishment when she perceived the nature of the challenge. "Marcus!" she gasped under her breath, "I can't be sitting next to *him*!"

But before his words could confirm her fears, they had reached her seat at table. The legendary personage next to whom she would presently dine greeted her with a flattering glance of great approval and a steady stream of conversation. The Duke of Wellington! This, indeed, was the moment of her greatest triumph. And she was surprised to find how very much she enjoyed it.

"Excuse the ignorance of a sheltered woman, Lord Wellington," Emma peered at him with intensity over the gold and crystal radiance of her sauterne, "but even you, a hero, must have felt fear at Waterloo—if only at the awesome task before you. Admit it, Lord Wellington, even heroes must feel fear," and she fluttered her lashes at his enchanted gaze.

"Ah, madame," the great warrior announced, taking

advantage of her compassion to grasp her darling little hand, "the clarity of your luminous gaze pierces my facade. How well you know the human heart. Yes, every man feels fear."

"But you, sir, and the glorious men who served under your command, seem to allow neither fear nor surprise to affect your actions. How I admire your performance in nipping that sneaky but spectacularly brilliant French charge in the bud . . . you must recall it . . . the second day, I believe."

"My dear lady, I am so flattered that *you* recall. But, surely, you were not there. How did you know?"

"Oh, from Marcus. Marcus Leicester," she smiled shyly at the Beau, who sat some distance down the table, fortunately, watching them. "Marcus has told me of your victories in great detail." And she thrilled as the Beau conscientiously returned her smile.

Wellington, acknowledging Marcus's attention by the rapid dropping of Emma's hand, responded rather poignantly, "Born lucky, that Leicester!" as he raised his glass and drank deeply, easing the ache of defeat.

Chapter XIV

"BUT, EMMA, DO you think he finds me . . . attractive?" The query was breathlessly addressed to our heroine one afternoon by her newfound friend, the effervescent Arabella Portney. The girl's bubbly nature was for the moment contained by the fact that Emma's peacock-feather and blue velvet gown was cut far too narrowly for the borrower's vivacious form. Standing before one mirrored wall of Emma's boudoir, poor, strapping Arabella saw what the apparently perfect front view concealed, a reflected view of a gaping expanse of underclothing.

"I think . . ." Emma reclined on the peach-and-cherry chaise, musing deeply. "I think . . . umm . . . yes, I think he finds you most attractive. And lively. But, perhaps, a bit too . . . too eager."

"Much too eager," intoned a voice from the bed. This note of sobriety issued from Arabella's sixteen-year-old sister, Caroline, lying next to a slumbering Barnaby, with her nose stuck in a book.

The younger sister's contribution caused Arabella to whirl around, not mindful of the unfastenable gown slipping down her front. "Caroline! You nasty little pig! How dare you!" In response, Caroline gave a brief snort and returned to her reading.

"Too eager?" Dispensing with the slip of a gown, Arabella returned it to its place in the wardrobe and moved on to a silvery-gray silk dressing gown, which, while it did not wrap intimately around her ample frame, at least met in front. As she preened and paraded, she pondered the point. "Too eager . . ." Suddenly, something in her thoughts startled her, and she looked away from the mirror and toward Emma, her expression grave. "Emma, when you say 'eager,' do you mean 'desperate?' Do you mean Harry Percy knows I have a . . . a *tendre* for him?"

Too quickly sister Caroline rushed in to fill Emma's polite silence with a jeering shout, "Does he know?" which she punctuated with hostile chortles. "Does he know!"

Casting her sister a savage glance, Arabella replied haughtily, "You are a hateful little worm, and if you do not proceed to crawl back into the earth where you belong, I shall report your hideous behavior to Mama upon our return home."

"Go ahead," dared the sister coldly from behind her book.

But she was soon forgotten, as Emma sat up and began to lecture her new love-sick friend. "Well, Arabella, I do think Harry is aware of your marital designs."

"But how? How could he?" Arabella threw herself down despondently on a chair too small to do her Junoesque presence the Olympian justice it deserved. "Oh, Emma, I adore him so. His ferocity! His temper! His passion! I dream that he will carry me away to his craggy Welsh castle and do with me the things they do not do in Miss

Austen's novels. Whatever they are." Too late, she cast a look at the sister who, although entranced in her book, was clearly committing to memory the entire colloquy. "And, Caroline, don't breathe a word of any of this to Mama or I shall come in the night and set your hair afire."

The younger girl, like the peach-beribboned animal beside her, chose not to respond.

"Oh," Arabella moaned, playing distractedly with the folds of Emma's gray gown as she crooned, "I must have him, Emma! No one will ever adore him as I do."

"Well, if that is true," Emma allowed, "you must realize that happiness is not in his nature. He is a warrior and must not be treated with the overzealous adoration reserved for fops or lap dogs. If I were you, I would reserve my blissful passion until after the ceremony."

As these words of womanly wisdom issued from her lips, the agreeable picture of Marcus teaching her restraint rose unbidden to her thoughts. I have grown so much under his tutelage, she realized with a pleasant start. And enjoy such better company. Imagine! The Lady Arabella Portney in my dressing gown, asking my advice in matters of the heart! And accepting it, it seemed; for Arabella sprang suddenly up from her chair, exclaiming, "Emma, you're right!" as she dashed back to the wardrobe.

"Oh dear!" she lamented. "If only I were your size!"

Contemplating Arabella's healthy, rosy prettiness, Emma was able to tell her, "Marcus Leicester says that Harry is a great fancier of the female forms painted by Rubens, which you do considerably resemble, Arabella dear."

"Oh, Marcus Leicester!" Arabella made abruptly as if to swoon. "Oh, Emma, how did you do it! He's the handsomest man in the world. And as if that weren't enough, it is well known that Lord Jason, too, has quite surrendered you his heart. How I envy you your two swains when I crave only the love of one man!"

Bound by her own web of secret oaths and grand designs, Emma could say nothing in explanation; she merely smiled a slight, enigmatic smile.

"But whom do you like the best, Emma? Which one will you choose?"

"Lord Jason," came the rapid reply, but not from Emma. At the very mention of the poet's name, Barnaby had awakened with a snarl, but Caroline, the speaker, was looking up from her book with a veritable purr. "Lord Jason!" the young girl repeated rapturously. "I am in love with his poem," she sighed, and clasping the treasured volume to her bosom, she leaped off the bed and ran to Emma. "Oh, Emma, his poem is so very wonderful. May I please borrow it? Please?"

Emma, from the lofty height of what seemed to the world to be consummate good fortune, graciously assented, "Yes, but be very careful with it."

"Oh, I will *treasure* it!" exclaimed the sullen brat, suddenly become a woman in love. "You must marry him, Emma, you must!"

And wondering if that was true, Emma looked for guidance to the great Barnaby who, as if weary of her dilemma, perversely proceeded to close his eyes and drift back to sleep.

The following day, hearing at least one voice, and possibly two, coming from within the pastel jade saloon, Emma was perplexed by the identity of the personage with whom Marcus Leicester might be conversing in her parlour before noon. Grasping the knob, she entered the room as quickly as possible, but even so, conversation had already ceased. To her amazement the room contained no second speaker, being occupied only by the Beau and Barnaby, who were seated opposite each other in postures of uneasy respect.

"With whom were you speaking, Lord Leicester?" she inquired, crossing to Barnaby and seizing him up in her arms.

"Speaking?" Marcus repeated. "Why, with no one, madame."

"But I was sure I heard your voice." Although her penetrating manner was intended to extract a confession, none was forthcoming. Looking down lovingly on the giant creature nestled in her arms, she cooed, "Barnaby, has Marcus been prying all my secrets out of you?"

In a gesture of disgust at the very idea of betrayal, Barnaby expressed a desire to descend, and when the floor had been attained, went loftily on his way.

But, unseen by Emma, as he swaggered from the room, he hastily turned his head back toward the Beau, bestowing a sort of a wink intended for Marcus's eyes only.

Chapter XV

ANNE GILLINGS SENSED with all her being that something was amiss this evening. Some half hour past, she had unaccountably been ordered to detain Lord Leicester in the *chinois* drawing room whilst Lady Emma completed her toilette without benefit of consultation.

That this abrupt new banishment had shaken the Beau as well as the servant was obvious from the distress which instantly clouded the blue-gray eyes. Despite his disappointment, Marcus surrendered to the lady's will and allowed himself to be led off to the newly refurbished parlor, where he settled into a brood. His musings were frequently interrupted by a glance at the chronometer which continued to inform him that, although the hour of ten fast approached, the lady's appearance did not seem imminent.

To his surprise, Marcus found his irritation growing with each fresh examination of the time. What in the world could be detaining her? Was she then, without him, in such a quandary over what to wear that they might never get to Almack's? Had her coiffure and *maquillage* been done again and again because she could not get it right?

Would she at last appear overdone, overdressed, over-painted, even less the elegant lady than she had appeared in their first encounter? Whatever gave her the notion that she could do without him? Did the snip of a girl bear the wild and wanton idea that she no longer required his instruction? And when she embarrassed herself, how then could he manage to convey the gravity of her error without abusing her sensibility? One hoped she would descend before the arrival of Lord Jason and be spared, at least, that further humiliation.

These thoughts provoked another glance at the time, and then a cigarette. Fifteen more minutes lumbered by, and then the ring of the doorbell announced to Marcus that the poet had arrived.

Now dressed in the very dinner clothes that Marcus and Brummell had introduced and all London had copied, Simon assumed a seat across from the Beau. Noting that his initial greeting had passed unnoticed, he called again. "Leicester! I say, old boy, what's troubling you?"

"Troubling me?" Marcus looked up from his trance. "Why nothing. Nothing at all," he snapped before sinking back into melancholy.

"And where is she?" Simon had just inquired when they heard the knob turn and saw the door opening.

"Emma!" Simon shouted first, rising at once from his chair.

Marcus declined to look toward the door, fearing the disaster that certainly awaited him there. Still, he must behave like the gentleman he was and he prepared to rise and confront her.

Emma, for her part, hesitated momentarily at the threshold as the door slowly swung open. Although now she could waft down the staircase on which lately she had stumbled, her spirit was far less steady than her step.

For the first time since Leicester's arrival, she had been dressed without his direction. For Almack's she had chosen a simple gown of mustard-golden shantung. Her coiffure, designed in collaboration by her and the resourceful Lucy, was likewise the essence of simplicity, drawn neatly back and worked into a bronze coil of an almost Chinese appearance, worn at the nape of her neck. A fresh, new understated *maquillage*, all innocent alabaster with a touch of pure, Chinese red at the cheeks and lips, had been created by the mistress and the maid. The dainty shantung slippers and red lacquer reticule were of Emma's own design, as was the *pièce de résistance*, a black satin cloak, richly embroidered like an Oriental village tapestry, with tiny houses and horses and people and streams. Against this magnificent garment, no gems, whatever their brilliance, could hold a candle, and so her only adornment was the vibrant auburn of her hair.

As she had turned for the last time before her mirror upstairs, Emma had felt a surge of pleasure in her appearance; she had managed it all without the aid of her adviser, and it was intended to shock, as much as to impress, him.

Now, however, as she attained the drawing room, her assuredness wavered, and she felt with a sinking certainty that she had misjudged herself. In an act of overweening pride, she had given her taste too much leeway, and now she would present herself both to Marcus and to Simon as a silly creature and an unfashionable fool. Still it was far too late to turn back.

Harsant, as always, stood outside the drawing room

door to admit her; as ever, his glance was inscrutable and gave Emma no hint of how she would be greeted by the beaux within. Having come this far alone, she must go yet farther, and once the door had fully opened, she moved lightly in to meet her well-deserved doom.

At the first sight of her, Jason sprang to his feet, as always, but failed to approach closer. Unspectacled as she was, she could not tell if his immobility derived from horror or delight. Marcus, of course, made no motion even to glance at her, but when he did, he too rose from his chair and stood quite still. Unable to ascertain either beau's reaction, Emma simply stood where she was, drowning in shame, praying the ground would open to swallow her up.

Something had to be done to end the awful silence, and taking the needful initiative, she strode toward the stricken escorts. Instantly they were animate once more, and Simon fairly sprinted to her side and grasped her hand.

"Emma!" he gasped, and, at close range, she could see in his regard, in his every gesture, her great, glorious victory. "Emma!" he repeated, unable to continue.

Gracefully she dropped his hand and took two small steps in Leicester's direction. "Lord Leicester," she began haughtily, gazing at the stationary figure, "tell me this gown will do for Almack's. It arrived only today, and I could not resist."

Clearing his throat tensely, Marcus managed to murmer, "Exquisite, madame," and then, "Exquisite!" once more.

His discomfiture marked the true extent of her triumph. In taking him by surprise, she had passed beyond his tutelage. Never again would he feel assured of his estimate of her capabilities. Never again would a sense of absolute dominance allow him to relax in her company. Wickedly, Emma wondered for a moment if his mysterious fiancée had ever reduced Marcus to his present state and, finally, joyously, doubted it. Secure in her victory, she turned away from the instructor as if he had been rendered invisible, and back toward her adoring Dante, as the most beatific of smiles illuminated her lovely face.

Chapter XVI

IN THE THREE weeks since her initial engagement, Emma had proved herself absolutely triumphant; but her continuing victories inspired even in Marcus a constantly renewed sense of wonderment, and respect. This day, for example, she had managed to captivate the four or five most notable gentlemen ever to host a Ladies' Tea at Watier's; moreover, upon her departure with Marcus, those gentlemen and many more had actually pursued her out the door and down the steps to the street. Even as Marcus was handing her into his carriage, the other gentlemen called out their adieus, each of which she delicately acknowledged with a smile and a word, reserving the most charming of waves for Lord Jason, who hung back, cloaked in an air of morbid desperation. " 'Til eight," she chimed to him, and he instantly brightened, acknowledging those delightful words with the lightest of kisses carried to her on the air from his fingertips. One last sparkling farewell for the assemblage, and off the couple flew, chattering and laughing gaily as their curricle raced down Pall Mall.

But once the romantic tableau had receded in the distance, the laughter ceased abruptly, to be succeeded by a solemn, "Well done, as usual, Lady Emma," on Marcus's part. She responded with a preoccupied nod. Then she lapsed into a silent musing, broken at last by a demand so sudden it caught him off guard.

"I want to practice walking by the river."

"Walking by the river? Now, madame? I would have to recommend against it. You've already had a most grueling afternoon, and it is well onto five. Would you not be better advised to return home to bathe and rest before Lady Cornwell's party?"

"Certainly not!" she countered energetically.

Surveying the greensward beyond him, Marcus had to admit that, spring having firmly settled in, London was looking especially fetching. Still, all his instincts urged him to return her to Belgrave Square. "Madame . . . ," he drawled disapprovingly.

"Lord Leicester," she sprang at him, "you are not my nanny. However, you are in my employ. And should I—let us suppose, tomorrow or next week—be walking along the river with Simon and do the wrong thing, just because you have been too weary to instruct me in the correct one, be assured my father shall hear of it!"

Spoiled brat! he fairly screamed, but he kept a manly silence, masking with benign concern his growing irritation with this constant companion.

It must be admitted that some part of that irritation was attributable to yet another new sensation: it was, he thought, confusion. Yes he was confused. For the first time in his gracious and perceptive life, Marcus Leicester was dealing with a woman he could not fathom. How, for instance, could the same girl be so utterly enchanting in company and so sullen and childish in private? And to him, of all people! The ingratitude of it quite took his breath away. Why, he alone had made her success possible!

It was this wild fluctuation in her behavior that stymied him. Even his own notoriously mercurial fiancée managed a certain consistency in her actions; but Emma knew no such restraints. And it was all so unreasonable; for as she had become more and more adept at public displays of affection, she had privately grown ever more cold and remote. He was quite unable to unearth the cause of her increasing distance from him, and his recent banishment from the boudoir had only served to cap his confusion.

Only after too many tossed and troubled nights did Marcus one early morning come bolt awake, the fugitive explanation at last imprisoned in his thoughts: she did not like him.

She did not like him! Clearly second in her esteem to that ass of a poet, Marcus was simply not up to Emma's bizarre standards. It had come to the point at which he could no longer ignore the truth of it. She found him both silly and dull, and consequently had begun to treat him with a vaguely hostile indifference, now that her successful come-out was assured. The little snip! How he would like to grab her up and hurl her into Jason's arms, where he was beginning to believe she belonged.

Would that one had not given one's word. Would that one could overcome the nearly irresistible urge to spank one's charge like the tantrumy child that she was. Would, dear God, that one were not a gentleman. But one was. And so, swallowing his pride, Marcus most amicably inquired, ''And where would madame like to promenade?''

''Oh,'' she answered without a moment's hesitation, ''on the Embankment, near your house; you promised we might promenade there. You haven't forgotten your promise, Lord Leicester?'' And she turned on him so insincerely cloying a glance that it chilled him.

"Of course, milady," he heard himself reply. "Your humble servant."

"Capital, Lord Leicester!" Her glee astonished him even more than her sharp comradely slap on his back. But neither was as shocking as her final gay exclamation. "And you must call me Emma!"

"Such a handsome couple!" This refrain had echoed down the Promenade for some quarter hour, apparently without attracting the notice of the objects of attention. Actually it was the manly half of the couple who seemed most unconscious of the scene around them. Just as, when they had first left off the carriage and started for the river across the road, he had failed to notice the innocent gray streak of cloud far in the west. Once they were embarked on the tour, Marcus's mood seemed to darken with the now lowering sky, which he never looked up to see. Furthermore the rapid dispersal of the passersby had eluded him, so that when the heavens opened, he was taken quite by surprise. Not so Emma, for whom each consequent difficulty perfectly suited her plan.

"Lord Leicester." She gently shook his arm. "It's raining!"

"Raining?" The word seemed foreign to him. "Raining?" Abruptly his eyes snapped back into focus, scanned the territory, and assumed a horrified look. "It's pouring! My God, Lady Emma, you'll be soaked! We must away! Quick, into the shelter of that copse." And, grabbing for the hand of his already sodden charge, he drew her quickly to a protected verdant glade beneath the trees. Removing his own moist jacket, he draped it over her streaming shoulders, then proffered his handkerchief so that she might dry her sodden coiffure.

"Have no fear, Lady Emma," he said spiritedly. "I feel sure the storm is merely a brief shower."

"Do you think so, Lord Leicester?" Having succeeded more in drenching the handkerchief than in drying her hair, Emma, lightly shaking the water from her curls, managed to gaze at him with a look whose charm could not completely disguise the mischief beneath. Smiling prettily, she suggested, "I wish I were as confident as you that the storm would pass quickly. I am troubled by that rumbling of thunder away in the west. It's bringing the storm right toward us, don't you agree? And see, where the wind's coming from." Marcus needed only one glimpse beyond the copse to realize that the sailor's daughter was correct. For he had often, at sea, witnessed this sort of quick approaching tempest which hit so suddenly that it caught even the saltiest of sailors unawares, and raged furiously on for hours afterward.

"Right you are, Lady Emma," he agreed jovially, restraining his extravagant desire to throttle her. "Right again!"

Since no further comment was forthcoming, Emma persevered. "And since we agree that the storm may not pass for hours, what do you suggest we do?"

"Do?"

"We can't stay here indefinitely. We'll both catch our deaths. I'm cold, and I believe you are trembling."

Granted, the muslin of his shirt was stuck fast to his dripping back, against which the chill rain continued to beat. Granted, the cold and the rain and the absolute loss of self-possession were propelling him further into painful inner turmoil. But never, never, would he ever tremble before a lady. As Emma had intended, this blow to his pride shook him back to his senses. "You're quite correct. We can't stay here." That seemed to be the extent of his plan.

"But where shall we go? My home is much too far. Where can we take shelter nearby? I urge you to think, Lord Leicester, of such a place before I am taken with the *ague*."

"Ah, yes. A place nearby." And as he suddenly paled, Emma knew she had led him perfectly into the trap.

"You seem to have hit on an idea, Lord Leicester," she sweetly urged, following with a distressing series of perfectly timed coughs.

"Oh, Lady Emma, you cough!" His concern seemed genuine.

"Do not be troubled by that, Lord Leicester. Although I have repeatedly sustained bouts of the *ague*, none has yet carried me off!" she allowed bravely.

"*Ague*? Repeated bouts?"

"Really, Lord Leicester, do not fear. My last attack kept me in bed for only two months, and for the last month, the physician had need to call only once a day."

"Oh." It was both a cry and a whisper.

Emma proceeded to launch another barrage of coughs, then ceased abruptly to exclaim as if spontaneously, "I know! *Your* house!"

"My . . . my house?" His shock was too clearly innocent to be feigned.

"Yes, Lord Leicester, *your* house. You live directly across the road, do you not?"

He nodded, hearing the hoofbeats of defeat fast approaching.

"Well," she snapped out the words like orders, "let us make a run for it. You do have fires in your house? Yes? And towels? Yes? And hot drinks? Lord Leicester, I am dying of the cold. Why do you object to seeing me safely conveyed indoors?"

"Ma—madame. I cannot permit you to be seen entering a gentleman's lodgings unchaperoned . . ."

"But who in the world will see us? They're all indoors themselves. And as for my being chaperoned, I presume your household staff can play some role in protecting my . . . reputation."

"At the moment there is no household staff," he admitted sheepishly.

"Whatever do you mean?"

"Eccentricity of mine. Give the staff, including my man Guillam, leave from three to nine every Sunday. Better for them, and no great matter to me, under . . . normal circumstances. But as it is, they won't return for hours." And as he sank back into his brood, the brat herself took matters in hand. "Well, then," she said firmly, staring him down, "we'll just have to risk it!"

Almost timidly he inquired, "Risk what, madame?"

"My reputation, Lord Leicester! I say, let's dash! And do make sure you've got the key!"

Chapter XVII

GREAT RAINDROPS FELL to the ground before them, exploding into lilliputian fountains, as Emma and Marcus raced across the road and up the flagstone path to Marcus's front door. There they paused while Marcus fumbled for his key.

That object was, at length, discovered nestled deep in the first pocket into which the Beau had looked; its unearthing caused in him a feeling far less bouyant than delight.

"Hurry, Lord Leicester! For I'm sure I shall faint from exposure any moment!"

The very notion of Emma's swooning dead away in his front doorway was enough to impel Marcus to secure entry to the house and draw milady in out of the rain with all possible haste.

"Oh!" Emma could not prevent herself from crying out, for before her eyes rose up the most charming of tiny round foyers. The glorious white curve of the room was accentuated by the crystalline radiance of the great chandelier, the stark black chinoiserie chairs placed against the walls, and the exquisite black and white marble tiles set into the floor underfoot. Great rectangular mirrors bordered in the same, narrow black lacquers as the chairs were intended to capture the images of every gorgeous lady and handsome gent who entered the house. Centered along the back wall, beneath the grandest mirror of all, stood a handsome curved lowboy of what appeared to be white lacquer, on top of which blossomed the most exquisite bouquet of cut spring flowers. To the right, a graceful covered staircase with a black railing insinuated its way to the mysteries waiting above and below. To the left towered a magnificently polished set of black double doors toward which Marcus was presently urging her.

Thankfully Emma felt her senses returning. The room was too stunning, much too disarming, by far. Even sodden and unspectacled, she was entranced by her own image reflected endlessly in the myriad mirrors and instinctively knew she would never look as wonderful as she did in this hall. Perhaps Marcus was a wizard after all! And this the evil castle to which he brought innocent girls for the purpose of ensorcelling them with their own vanity. And, having ensorcelled them . . . her fearful fancies nearly caused her to shudder anew. Thrusting her fear aside, she more gently reminded him, "Lord Leicester, I am soaking wet and am loath to drip all over your study. You might first provide me with a towel with which to dry myself." But her cautionary words did not deter him from leading her through the ebony doors.

"The rug near the fire is fur," he explained, "and has long been used to the elements. Now come here by the blaze which Guillam, an unfailing prognosticator of storms, must have put up before his departure."

Marcus was right, for within the black marble fireplace sparkled the most golden of friendly little fires—intended to burn just long enough to warm the chilled victim of a sudden April shower.

Marcus escorted her toward the rug, on which he invited her to recline as she warmed herself. She did as she was told, enjoying the luxury of toasty hands and feet as she surveyed the fabulous study: deep China-red walls, black straight-leg armchairs, sofa and tables, all exhibiting a stark yet appealingly masculine simplicity of taste, the room made splendidly comfortable by colorful Oriental rugs, and bright cushions and fur throws casually arranged on the floor and couches.

The dusk and rain had combined to bring the sun down before half past six and the only bright light in the room came from the dazzle of the fire and the glow of the oil lamps set in brass wall sconces and upon the tables.

"Well now!" As he spoke, Marcus strolled past an impressive wall of bookcases to the huge windows over-looking the river, pulled shut the draperies, and continued on to a lacquered wardrobe. Thence he proceeded, once it was opened, to search until he dispelled the mystery by exclaiming, "Ah, here it is!" And he extracted from its depths a large striped dressmaker's box. He brought the present to her and begged her to open it.

Within the box, Emma discovered to her breathless delight, was a most precious and remarkable lady's dressing gown of richest sapphire-blue velvet. It was completely lined with the ermine that bordered its cuffs and hem and its compressed huge, warm collar.

"For me?" she asked in astonishment as he lifted it out of the box and held it up for her. Realizing that he knew it was not her color, she now fathomed the plain fact that the gift was intended for another; and, somewhat deflated, she inquired, "Will it fit me?"

"Well . . . ," he stammered. "It is actually a gift for my sister, but surely . . ."

Despite his evasions, every female instinct told Emma that the robe she would soon be wearing was intended not for his sister at all but for the unspeakable fiancée. Despite his generosity, that perception provoked a return of the annoyance she had not felt in hours.

"And how do you propose I dry my clothing?" she responded sharply. "You must be an expert at that."

Dropping the box on the floor and throwing the robe on one of the fireside chairs, Marcus helped Emma to her feet as he announced with a maximum of *bonhomie*, "Speaking as an officer and a veteran of the campfire, I would suggest standing two of these cane chairs with their backs toward the hearth and then draping the sodden garments over them, facing the fire. If one takes care to secure the proper distance to avoid scorching, it is a quick and dependable way of drying garments."

The fact that she would rather die than wear his fiancée's robe was now overshadowed by her sense that she would rather wear Bonaparte's own dressing gown than remove her dress before Marcus. But just as she had decided the clothes must dry on her, the Beau-Nanny broke in, "I am off to the kitchen to prepare us both a hot drink. My absence will assure you all the time you require to change. Tea or coffee? Coffee? Yes?" And before she could reply, he vanished through the ebony doors.

"Coffee, it is." Marcus called out this announcement some ten minutes later as he kicked open the double doors to display a laden tray. Having spent some time arranging herself, styling her posture after his own instruction, Emma was pleased to note that her efforts seemed to have stopped him in his tracks in the doorway.

Seated languidly on the fur rug by the crackling fire,

reclining against a pyramid of patterned cushions, Emma had draped the folds of the gown in so perfectly flattering a fashion that the velvet seemed to glow upon her body as it caught the firelight. The ermine hem was drawn artfully up to allow only a modest view of the delicate feet, and the huge ermine collar pushed high, so that her drying auburn curls, released from all restraint, tumbled freely over the collar and down her back. She had turned her face toward the fire in such a way that its warmth gave her skin the sheen of pink alabaster.

Her own garments, hanging before the fire, per Marcus's suggestion, had begun to dry and, as he continued to stare at her from the doorway, she reached out a hand to ascertain their progress.

"Still damp." She eased back onto the cushions, and then pertly inquired, "And what wonders are you bearing on that salver?"

"Oh, nothing terribly exotic. It is a blend of coffee beans from Africa and America, roasted and ground by my man Guillam, and brewed to his specifications. Here are some of his legendary chocolate buns as well, should you be hungry. And this is the finest cognac ever to be free-traded from France." As he bore the tray to a low table near Emma, she noticed that he, too, had changed his clothing. He now wore plain gray trousers of a light flannel fastened at the waist with a narrow leather belt. His open-necked shirt was of light plaid of the new Madras cotton over which he wore an odd collarless jacket of supple yellow knitted fabric, with buttons down the open front. On his feet were red stockings and flat black slippers.

"May I inquire as to the nature of your jacket?" Emma asked.

"Ah, the jacket. Yes, this is a little something," he smiled, "that Brummell and I have been working on for some time now. Almost had Lord Cardigan interested in it for his regimental gear, but he claimed the army wasn't ready for such dandyism. Still hoping, though," he chuckled as he prepared the coffee for her.

"I think you'll find this to your liking," he said as he looked over the tray and down at her, still smiling. "Just a dollop of Devonshire cream and two lumps of Jamaica raw sugar, and to encourage the warmth back into your chilled bones, a little cognac." Having poured the fiery golden liquid into a snifter, he warmed it with his hands, then took the glass in one hand and the cup and saucer in the other and, crossing to her and kneeling down, placed both on a tiny lacquered footstool he had first edged with his foot to her side.

Returning her genuinely amiable smile with a rather thin-lipped one of his own, he returned to the tray and the preparation of his coffee. "A cake?" he inquired. As she declined, he picked up his own glass and cup and moved rather warily to a chair opposite her.

Inhaling the heady perfume of the brandy, Emma raised her glass toward Marcus, who responded in kind, and she convivially pledged, "To your sister!"

Not until the brandy was cascading down his throat did Marcus realize what he had toasted, and the dreadful perception brought on a strong fit of coughing.

"Why, Lord Leicester, whatever is wrong?"

"It's nothing, Lady Emma!" Only with heroic effort could Marcus subdue himself. "Nothing at all," he proclaimed, when at last he could speak calmly. "Unless, perhaps . . . I have fallen victim to your own recent illness."

Gazing innocently up at him, Emma suggested, "In truth, I have been told that the possibility of contagion does exist in such cases as mine. And further, that once having struck, the illness is difficult to shake. But rest assured, it is the kind of condition in which there is far less pain than discomfort.''

Suddenly aware that by sitting forward in his chair he was drawing very near to her, Marcus bolted upright and consumed the brandy in a gulp. He rose and brought the decanter to the waiting glass on the table beside him. As he poured and quaffed a second brandy, Emma, having learned from bitter experience to sip slowly, thought to suggest that her teacher recall this lesson himself, but she merrily decided against it. Her secret merriment increased as he drew out his handkerchief to mop the suddenly moist brow.

''Are you warm, Lord Leicester?'' The concern in her tone could not, even by an expert, have been pronounced anything but genuine.

His eyes darted to the large windows, behind which the storm could still he heard. ''Warm?'' He seemed so surprised by the question as to be hard put for an answer. ''Not warm, but—'' he seized a moment to study the point ''—warm*er*,'' and then proceeded to polish off yet a third brandy.

Whatever the liquor's restorative properties, it had done little to bring back the color to cheeks growing increasingly pallid, nor had it served to assuage his palpable unease. He was weakening, thought Emma, precisely according to plan. After weeks of waiting and strategizing, the glorious moment had arrived when she would exact her tribute, and her revenge.

Quietly she played with her brandy glass and then, raising her eyes to meet his elusive gaze, she requested sweetly, ''Might I interrupt this moment of meditation to solicit your professional advice on a somewhat urgent matter?''

That Emma seemed prepared to steer them back into the

safer waters of business caused Marcus to relax a little. "With pleasure, Lady Emma."

"All right then, if you've no objection." Emma felt her heart beat faster in anticipation. "Try not to be shocked with the intimate confidences I must share with you now," she continued, and paused just long enough to see in his face the anxious speculation that her suggestive words had produced.

"Oh, Lord Leicester, you need not appear so distressed. I am not promised, if that is what worries you. But I may be, soon, assuming your expert instruction continues."

She sensed he intuited something, and the feeling was confirmed when he uneasily demanded, "Any particular kind of instruction, madame?"

Emma was prepared to take her time. "Actually yes. Lord Leicester—I feel that, given the nature of our present conversation, it is only fitting that you call me Emma, and I call you Marcus. Agreed?"

Suspicion replaced anxiety in his troubled countenance; nevertheless, hoping to hurry her on to the point, he readily agreed. "Certainly . . . Emma . . . ."

"Now, Marcus," and she let his name linger on her lips as she rose to her knees, facing him in the pose of Dignity the Supplicant. "Although I am ashamed of . . . oh, well, you, see . . . oh!" And she forced out an odd little chirp before continuing more directly. "To speak frankly, there is something I have never done with a man which I am impelled to learn instantly."

Fortified by yet another brandy, the stricken Beau managed only a weak half-response. "What would that . . . ?"

As he could not seem to go on, Emma leaped in again.

"There is something I must learn, and learn now, and you are the only man in a reasonable position to teach it to me. Lord Leic—Marcus, before this evening ends, you must teach me to kiss."

She refused to let his shocked silence answer for him. "Well, Marcus? You seem . . . reticent."

"Reticent? Why no. But . . . it's impossible, your request. Impossible." And he lapsed into further silence which, however, he was able to breach with an inspired idea. "It's simply impossible, you see, because . . . because Guillam may be back any second."

"You said he wouldn't return until nine." Still she fixed him with her innocent stare. "Isn't that so?"

Marcus had drawn his hands together in what appeared less a clasp than a wringing. "No, you see, I forgot. When it rains, he always returns at seven. Guillam especially worries about my welfare in bad weather!" Considering himself safe at last, Marcus grew noticeably cheerier as he continued, "And it must already be well onto the hour—"

"Nonsense, Marcus. Look up at the clock on your own mantel. It struck six only some ten minutes past."

"Ten past six," Marcus muttered, "how could it be only . . . ?"

"So, Lord Leicester, we've plenty of time. When your man returns, I will already be well tutored and safely on my way home. Let's not waste a moment. If Lord Jason intends, as I believe he does, to kiss me this very evening, I must garner all the instruction I can right now. Come on! It's only a job of work." And, rising to her full height, she extended her arms to him.

For one moment more his will held, then she felt him capitulate. As proof of her victory, he rose slowly to his feet, allowing her to take one limp hand in hers and walk him to the fire, where she dropped his hand and moved opposite, as she had done so many times when they danced.

From her greatly inferior height, she looked up to find his eyes distractedly scanning the ceiling. "Marcus! Lord Leicester! How do we proceed?"

Lowering his eyes unexpectedly to meet her own, he

gave the smallest jump backward, as if he had been startled by a loud noise. "Yes . . . proceed . . . well . . ." As she had said, a job of work was a job of work; that was his only possible justification. In as cool and masterful a tone as he could command, he began the lesson. "First, let's assume the same posture we do for the waltz. Now, I retain one arm lightly around you, just so . . . but—"

Her enthusiasm overtook his measured instructions. "I know! You'll drop my hand, like this! Then draw your free arm about me, until it almost meets the other. Is that correct? Like so." As gracefully as she could, given his refusal to relax, she maneuvered him into position.

"Very good," he murmured weakly.

"Now, Marcus," she purred like a jungle cat, "if I've guessed correctly, I must place my arms, likewise, around you." And to bear out her opinion, she gently raised her hands until the palms hovered some infinitesimal distance from him. Next, almost swooning with the ecstacy of combat, she allowed her hands, without touching him, to trace the circumference of his body, until they met, mere inches from his back.

"Should I touch you now?" Her words were muffled by the fabric on his chest.

"Should I?" she demanded once more, but receiving no response, decided to do so anyway. As her hands rested lightly on the thin wool jacket, she could feel beneath it the stern presence of his spine and the graceful muscles rippling away on either side of it.

Suddenly she felt his grasp on her tighten. The fingers of his hand kneaded the fabric of her robe and her skin beneath while, with the other hand, he tenderly caressed her head, urging it dreamily backward, then bent over her, and found her more than willing mouth with his own.

Withdrawing his lips for half a passage of time, he murmured, "Emma . . ." As he bent down again toward

134

her, Emma was hurled into a giddy spiraling of delight. And just as her pleasure began to cloud her recollection of the game she played, there came a knocking on the door, followed by an urgent call.

"Lord Leicester, sir. Are you in there?"

Quite beside himself, Marcus sprang back from Emma and whispered urgently, "Guillam! By God, he's returned!"

"He can't have!" Emma insisted futilely, hastily rearranging her curls and her robe. "It's not yet half past six."

"I told you he'd be back," Marcus insisted, though in fact his surprise was as great as her own.

Again came the pounding and shouting, to which, in desperation, Marcus finally replied, "Guillam, old man. I'm quite fine. Just taking a bit of a lie-about!"

"Shall I enter, then, sir?" shouted the manservant.

"No!" shouted Marcus. "I mean, no, don't bother." He waited a moment. "I'd like a minute or so to collect myself," Marcus called out less frantically, punctuating his remarks with an operatic yawn. "Be in my chambers in five minutes," he called as he ran frantically about, hurling the contents of Emma's glass and cup into the fire, then burying glass, cup, saucer, and spoon under the mound of cushions. Last, he replaced the drying chairs and was about to hand Emma her clothes, when Guillam spoke again, "And will you be wanting a bath, sir?"

"No bath, Guillam." Marcus was straightening himself up as he spoke, knowing Guillam would greet him with an eagle's eye. "I must go out posthaste."

"The weather is very poor, sir," the infernal man intoned disapprovingly.

"No matter, Guillam."

"As you say, sir, and my apologies for awakening you." It was evident from the servant's tone that he little believed and condoned less his master's version of recent

135

events. And although he had conceded to depart, he remained outside the door awaiting the emergence of Marcus—and whomever else from the study.

"Here!" Marcus whispered, throwing Emma her garments. "Hide behind the curtains until I depart the room. Then, when I have secured Guillam in my chamber, you can throw the robe and the box in the wardrobe, slip out the front door, and wait for me across the road."

"But it's still pouring! I'll get soaked again!"

As he moved slowly, softly toward the door, he turned to her and whispered *sotto voce* but with great conviction, "Madame, remember: no price is too great for the preservation of a lady's reputation." And without further ado, after motioning her to take cover, Marcus passed through the door, leaving Emma, stunned and blushing, to question the veracity of his opinion.

Chapter XVIII

"BUT IF YOU find him—your word, Emma—'stuffy' . . .
then why are you always in his company?" Simon hissed
at the lady on his arm, his tone the customary admixture of
venom and bewilderment when the subject was Marcus.

Before responding to his heated demand, Emma blew a
kiss across the ballroom at her best friend, Arabella Portney,
who, having taken her confidante's sage advice, was bravely
attempting to restrain her ebullience as she strolled through
Almack's with her darling, dour Harry Percy.

"Emma! Emma, answer me!" Simon insisted. Without
removing her gaze from the glittering assemblage, Emma
shortly replied, "He is not always stuffy, Simon." To
emphasize her further point, she turned at last toward him,
"And he is so persistent."

"Emma, I do not believe for a moment that Leicester
would continue to make a pest of himself if you discouraged him. You disparage him constantly, but you never
discourage him. I simply do not comprehend."

"Oh, pish, Simon!" was Emma's tart reply. But in her heart was raging a far more frenzied confusion.

Since that fateful afternoon of the kissing lesson, her relations with her tutor had assumed an uneasy formality which had never before colored their time together.

In the fine days before her transformation was complete, they had laughed as she learned, joked when she tripped, applauded when she succeeded. Now there was neither good humor nor celebration. Whereas then he had warmly grinned his approval, now he acknowledged her small triumphs with a stern-lipped almost military strictness. Their morning reviews of her previous evening's performance had always before been laced with gossip and amusing anecdotes; now he arrived a full hour later than before, critiqued her succinctly in the downstairs sitting room, and hastily withdrew. Surely he must be as uncomfortably aware as she that suddenly neither them had any conversation at all.

Perhaps this new behavior was an acknowledgment that their time together was drawing to an end. For her goal was well within sight. In a matter of weeks, or days, Simon would propose marriage at last, and she would have what she most desired.

In truth, Marcus Leicester had earned not only his salary, but her sincerest gratitude as well. And yet it was that very gratitude she could not help but withhold from him when they were together. Such were her thoughts as she walked with her suitor to the refreshment table. As Simon bent over the Scotch salmon, indicating to the servant his lady's pleasure, Emma recognized Marcus across the room, his back to her, deep in conversation with a distinguished lady of a certain age.

So gracious was his manner, so comely his presence, that Emma could not remove her eyes from him. To her astonishment, he seemed to feel her gaze upon his back,

presence for an indeterminate period of time . . ." Her voice trailed off as she was struck by visions of just what the Beau might be doing. "But there's more," she compelled herself to continue briskly. "Let me read on . . ."

As Emma studied and Sir Anthony fairly panted with adoration, Simon chose the moment to review his newly considered strategy. The desperation of his financial position had forced him to escalate his siege upon Lady Emma just when the arrival of Leicester had made it almost impossible for anyone to be alone with her long enough to pop the question. Leicester was always at her side, although whether by her desire or no Simon could not tell. Sometimes Emma seemed irritated by Leicester to the point of fury; often, however, she seemed to glow when he so much as touched her arm. Simon had, certainly, warned her that the man was after her fortune; but there was no evidence that she had taken the advice to heart. And now, just when Leicester was momentarily out of the picture, Anthony Chase had arrived to replace him as an even more dangerous rival. For while Leicester was after her fortune, and might be seen through, Chase, securely well set up on his own, was undoubtedly interested only in her heart. So maddened with desire was the former rake that he might be inflamed to the point of suing for her hand. With Leicester gone, Chase, too, would seek to strike at once. To win his suit, Simon would have to take a page from the Beau's primer. As Marcus kept always to Emma's side, so Simon would, and, by this time next week, pending only the father's assent (and that was assured), the lady and the fortune would be his.

As the poet meditated, Sir Anthony cast a huge, puppy-dog smile at Emma. "Given your permission, Lady Emma, I would be most honored to be allowed to accompany you both to the route party."

Seeking to squelch Chase's most unsatisfactory proposal

before Emma could agree, Simon intervened, "So sorry, old man. Lady Emma has already consented to be my partner at dinner before the event."

"Dinner?" Emma began, but her seeming demurral was interrupted by Simon, who once again addressed his new rival with new hauteur. "Very small party . . . so sorry . . ."

Disappointed but undefeated, Sir Anthony proposed instead to meet up with them later at Lady Melbourne's.

Once that compromise had been agreed to, both gentlemen rose to depart. Before retreating from the room, however, they strode to Emma for the obligatory kiss to the hand.

"Oh my!" Emma was tucking Leicester's missive in her sleeve when a distressing thought occurred to her. "Marcus was to convey to me my mask for the Vauxhall event of Thursday next. If he's not coming, I won't have it for my fitting tomorrow. Oh drat!"

"Perhaps, milady," Anthony Chase suggested, "you could send for it."

"Yes, I suppose I could," Emma murmured.

" 'Til tonight, then." Simon rushed to appropriate her hand, which he pressed to his lips, before grudgingly surrendering it to Chase's waiting paw.

" 'Til seven!" Simon specified as he proceeded to the door, followed by Chase who, taking one last lingering look at his beloved, himself sighed, " 'Til tonight!" and departed.

Alone once more, Emma had occasion to reflect on the fact that Simon's temperament had, finally, become inflamed beyond reckoning. At last the fleshly poet was become one with the poet of her dreams. But that task of triumph was flavored with rue, for deep in her soul she fought against a growing realization that the dreams signified much less since that day with her tutor in the rain. As she extracted and examined Marcus's disturbing note, the terrible irony of her situation forcefully presented itself to her. For Marcus, a master of provoking passion in others, had not the power to encourage it in his own nature. He was, manifestly, a cold fish, and God pity his fiancée, whoever she was!

Suddenly Emma wanted to know the mysterious temptress's identity more urgently than she had ever craved anything before. She would know! And now! By tonight, when Simon might propose, she must discover the several things Marcus was too much of a gentleman ever to have told her. And no sooner had she thus determinedly vowed then a plan sprang into her feverish brain. Congratulating herself upon her own infernal cleverness, she ran in search of Lucy, who was discovered in her little garret room, arranging her hair.

"Ma'am!" the girl cried, startled by the sight of her mistress; but she recovered herself when Emma urgently whispered, "Lucy, we must talk!"

Once the door was closed again behind the two conspirators, words flew and events proceeded quickly. In less than fifteen minutes, by the little clock over Lucy's dressing table, mistress had become maid.

"I swear, madame, you look better in my things than I do!" Lucy laughed merrily. "Just remember, ma'am, you must not speak like a lady. You've got to talk like me. Haitches as broad as ye please, and so on. Your appearance'll never give you away, but your *tony* accent might."

"*I* know!" Emma paused in the midst of arranging Lucy's somber little cloak around her. "I'll speak with a French accent. The servingman will thus think me a foreigner and hopefully refrain from idle conversation."

"Perfect, ma'am! Well, you'd best be off, for the hour is almost four."

"So I must, Lucy," announced the newest serving girl

in Belgrave Square. "So I must," she chirped again and went skippingly down the stairs to her latest adventure.

Fortunately the afternoon was balmy, and Emma's voyage of discovery was launched in the pleasantest of climates. Her head spun both with exhilaration and dread as she made her way to Chelsea, down Bywater Street, and along the King's Road until she turned off toward Cheyne Walk. Would she find her worst fears confirmed—whatever they might be? And if she continually failed to give form to those fears, how could she possibly envision the reality? What did she want from Marcus? And, even were that decided, the question of whether he wanted anything at all from her remained to be answered. All answers awaited her, tantalizingly, within the mysterious upstairs chambers in Cheyne Walk, toward which her steps now, perhaps fatally, carried her.

Striding boldly up the walk to the door of that house, she screwed up her courage and rang the bell.

The door opened to reveal a small bald figure, garbed in a costume halfwise between an admiral's uniform and a butler's rig. A look of natural condescension possessed his face, as he inquired haughtily, "Yes?"

First giggling charmingly, then breaking into a most heavily French-accented English, she stumbled, "I am zee maid of Ledee Emma Davenant, and I 'ave come for zee masque."

"But I haven't yet picked it up, girl. Lady Emma should even now be receiving a missive to the effect that it is to be brought to her home at seven. Why are you here now?" He was, very evidently, looking down his nose at her, although their eyes were, in fact, level.

Emma was not to be put off. "*Mais oui, monsieur*. Madame read a note, then summon me an' order me here to peek up zee masque. *Et voici*, here am I!"

"I've just told you, foolish girl, that someone has erred.

144

Be so good as to return to your home and report that the mask will be delivered." As he was about to close the door on her, she burst into a remarkable shower of tears.

"Oh monsieur, pleeze not to send me back wizout eet! Ze butler ees so cruelle to me, and so iz Madame Gillings." Seeing through her tears that the very threat of a lady's hysterics at the front door was making the servant uneasy, she persevered. "Pleeze, sir, help me!" she wailed and wept the harder, at which he bowed to decorum and hastily escorted her inside, closing the door behind her lest the neighbors hear her sobs.

As her misery continued, the manservant, half in desperation and half out of a natural sympathy he could never contain for long beneath his gruff exterior, led her to one of the ebony side chairs and went so far as to proffer his handkerchief.

Seizing the cloth with apparent gratitude and bringing it at once to her streaming eyes, she pleaded with him. "Oh, *monsieur, s'il vous plaît*, you must to fetch zee masque and bring eet back here so I do not return—'ow you say?—hopen-'anded'? I beg you, *monsieur*. Eef I were dismissed, I should not know what to do." And, as at the very thought, a fresh burst of tears broke loose.

"All right, all right!" the stern yet gentle little man exclaimed at last. "If you'll stop that crying, I'll go fetch the mask right now. You sit right here; I will be back in no more than ten minutes. But cease that weeping," he ordered, and, rubbing his forehead distractedly, he crossed to the stairs, which he descended, and was gone.

Scarcely a moment passed before Emma, praying she would not be discovered by some other servant, raced to the staircase and followed its spiral upward. She found herself in a small hallway, beyond which ran a long corridor with a door at the end. Instinct instructed her to follow the corridor, and she did, running all the way, then grasping and turning the door handle, which gave easily. She quietly closed the door behind her and leaned momentarily against it, almost panting with relief at having thus far evaded detection.

So great was that relief that it took Emma a moment to recover herself sufficiently to survey the scene before her. Surely fortune had guided her footsteps, for this room could only be his bedchamber.

It was, quite unlike the cool elegance of the downstairs chambers, a vision out of the *Arabian Nights*. The walls were hung with the most lavishly colored rugs and draperies. Carpets of myriad designs blanketed the entire floor, their bright opulence echoed by gorgeous velvets and silks that canopied the fur-covered bed. So sensually delightful a place Emma had never even imagined, and a feeling of the most intense pleasure, compounded with no small trembling of fear, washed over her. Here was a room so overwhelming in its luxury that its very existence threatened a lady's virtue. Emma knew she must instantly set about her mission and quickly, quietly return to her place in the downstairs hall.

Nestled in a corner of the candlelit room was a small desk and it was toward this bastion of masculine privacy that Emma was drawn. Sure enough, through her unspectacled haze, she made out a pen, inkwell, and sheet of paper plainly laid out on its surface.

Approaching cautiously and bending over the paper to see what might be written there, she felt her heart pounding with excitement.

But what she saw thrust her almost bodily from the table and propelled her across the room, through the door, along the corridor, and down the steps; when she resumed her seat to await Guillam's return, her horror was still too profound to allow for so easy an outlet as tears. The worst had happened, no, worse than the worst. In the time it had taken her to unpuzzle the scrawl on the page, her existence had been immediately shattered. For written in his own hand were the most hideous words in the world: "My dearest Florissa."

Chapter XX

NOT HAVING SEEN his Emma in the three days since she had declined the route party, Simon was shocked at her present appearance.

At the time her pleas of illness had seemed a frivolous camouflage for some mysterious lady's brood. But now, seeing the light fled from her eyes, the distressing chalkiness of her complexion, and the listlessness of her demeanor, the poet wondered if his prey were not truly and gravely stricken.

"Emma," he asked with the profound concern of the greedy. "Emma, whatever is the matter?"

It seemed to him that briefly she was close to tears, but suppressed them with a sigh and murmured pallidly, "Nothing, Simon. It's just . . . you know . . . a megrim." And with that, her words trailed off.

"Can I do something, dear Emma? Can I fetch you a refreshment? Some tea, perhaps?" He crossed to her and took her indifferent hand.

"Yes, Simon, that would be nice. Why don't you ring for Harsant?"

He jumped up and as he ran to the door, called, "I'll just tell him directly. Seems faster," and he rushed away, clearly made uneasy by his lady's afflicted state.

Relieved of the necessity of making conversation, Emma returned to the private despair in which she had dwelt since the revelation of Marcus's terrible secret.

On the morning following that fateful event, he had sent another note round to her. Emma had not been able to peruse it for the pain that pierced her when she tried, but Lucy had slowly and correctly read out as many of Leicester's lies as Emma could stand before she halted the recitation.

Summoned out of London on an urgent errand, he had announced. A matter which could not be postponed. Return highly uncertain for the next week or so.

She despised him more, at that moment, for the lies than for the deeds they masked. She hated him for leading her on, and astray. She despised him for choosing the way of the *ton* over grace, and dazzle over dignity, never reminding herself that her rival had preceded in Marcus's affections. Most of all, she loathed him for giving her a sliver of time of sheer delight and then abruptly, cruelly, snatching it from her.

In response to his latest note, Emma, calling upon her little remaining pride, composed a terse and toneless missive to the effect that she would no longer be requiring Marcus's services. And she silently vowed that, should he return precipitously to Belgrave Square, should he implore her to receive him, she would never agree. She would never, *never* see him again, even in the unlikely circumstance that Florissa allowed it.

But how could she possibly recover from his terrible betrayal when every room of her house bespoke his presence? Living alone in the big house was impossible: she would die here! She had to get away. That was the solution, certainly. By the time Simon returned, a wonderful plan had seized her imagination.

"Tea will be along, dear Emma," Simon offered with solicitude. "And, I must say, you appear suddenly much improved."

"Yes, Simon, I *am* much improved." Emma's cheerier tone gave Simon renewed hope for their joint future. "But it has occurred to me," she announced, "that a weekend in the country will quite cure me. I've heard of a perfectly delightful little inn in Devon; it would be just the thing. Let's round up Arabella and Harry and Anthony Chase and all our servants and depart at once!"

"But, Emma," Simon hesitated, chilled at the thought of this unforeseen expenditure. Nevertheless it might be a worthy investment, as it were. His mood brightened at the thought. "A splendid idea, Emma," he crowed. "Simply splendid!"

"Yes, I think it is the perfect thing. Let me call for pen and paper and send invitations to our several friends! Let's see . . . oh, and Barnaby must come as well!"

Simon stifled his disgust and agreed. "Absolutely, Emma. Idea's simply top of the trees!"

"Oh Simon," Emma crowed, "I think this escapade will alter all our lives!"

So saying, she was struck by the miraculous fact that not for three whole minutes had she thought of Marcus.

Chapter XXI

HIGH SPRING REIGNED over the posy-covered Devon hills, and warm breezes flitting from the perfect blue of the sky brushed against the group of travelers like silk against bare skin.

Any walker in the meadows would certainly have noted for repetition at his own fireside the gay and elegant caravan progressing through the countryside. Further, such an observer might have savored for comment the superior appearance of the four carriages, as well as the graceful mounts who led them; the plethora of baggage requiring a carriage of its own; the demure pastoral charm of the ladies' muslin frocks trimmed, like their bonnets, in ribbons of the purest pastels; the tasteful display of colors bright enough to match the season of the jovial gentlemen's attire. And, finally, the passerby would have been able to inform the party, had they stopped to ask, that their idyllic destination lay only moments away.

As the first of the carriages, a black curricle, achieved the crest of a hill, its passengers were rewarded with a vision of surprising loveliness.

"Oh my," Emma exclaimed, catching sight of the perfect little Tudor inn no great distance before them. "Simon, isn't it sweet! How clever of Marcus to have known of it!"

The hateful name had slipped unbidden from her careless lips; its articulation caused Simon momentarily to take his eyes from the road and piercingly examine her own.

"Marcus? What has Marcus Leicester to do with this?"

"Nothing! Nothing at all. It is just that, until this very moment, I had quite forgotten it was Marcus who first told me of the place. That's all." Emma's regret at having now recalled the fact was intense.

Simon had turned his attention back to the road, but his tone remained sharp. "Were you with him here, Emma? Is this where he brought you when you left London together? Is this the nature of the pain to which you intend to subject me? Must I be haunted by the words he may have whispered, the fields through which you might have strolled . . ."

"Oh, Simon, stop this at once! It is very foolish." Emma's pain was increased by her companion's ignorant evocation of cherished memories which would never, in fact, be hers. "I have not visited this place before, and that is that!"

Her words caused Simon's mood suddenly to shift. Removing one hand from the reins, he employed it to seize Emma's (taking care to avoid the maw of Barnaby, curled warily in his mistress's lap).

"My dear Emma," he veritably cried out, "forgive me, forgive my anger, forgive my jealousy. I quite forgot myself. Forgive me."

"Of course, Simon," Emma murmured, allowing her hand to be dropped as she mused on the recent course of this romance. Just as you said it would happen, Marcus, just as you taught me, she thought wryly, then forced her spirits to busy themselves as the inn itself was achieved.

Simon's man having preceded the party hence to settle the arrangements, our travelers retired almost immediately into the charming arms of country luxury.

After having been shown their most cheerful and flowery chambers, they all repaired to a downstairs parlor of glowing wooden furniture and colorful fabrics of a thousand flowers. Merry light streamed in the windows, beyond which a brook babbled and fields playfully twisted this way and that to the boundless blue sky.

The hostlers, a jolly French couple of middle-age, displayed an ample girth as advertisement for their cuisine, and soon a veritable feast was laid before the famished voyagers.

Here, for the Londoners' pleasure, were trays of country pâtés, of partridge, rabbit, goose, and pheasant, studded with nuts and raisins or worked into grand patterns of color and texture. Here were great loaves of bread still hot from the oven, accompanied by fresh-churned butter in crockery tubs. A perfectly roasted fowl with Cumberland sauce and a smoked country ham sat in state upon the massive table. Pickled legumes of every variety, relishes sweet, sour, and hot, and mustards of many hues and flavors were available for the dressing and enlivening of the main courses.

There were fresh lettuces and scallions dressed in shallot vinegar and a delightful oil, olives, and cornichons, radishes, and tiny tomatoes. Should the diner crave still more variety, there was a piquant salad of green beans, an indescribably succulent one of potatoes, and another of ruby beets and tiny pearl onions. A magnificent arrangement of early summer fruit was surrounded by great wheels of cheese both delicate and rich. Tarts of apple and berry, complemented by fresh whipped cream, were conveyed to a sideboard as the meal progressed, and as if this did not suffice for delightful sweetness, there appeared as well little iced cakes of many shapes and colors, and great bowls of pudding. To soothe the overstimulated palate, chilled cider flowed freely. The feast, presented upon a snow-white cloth, was served on huge plates of a country floral design.

Happily attended by the hostler and his wife, the guests ate and joked and planned their days ahead. Finally, after crying, "Enough!" Anthony Chase announced his intention to seek his chamber for a nap. Following his lead, Barnaby achieved a sunny snoozing spot outside the door in a patch of marigolds that matched the hue of the ribbon around his neck.

The morose Harry Percy characteristically retreated into the relative gloom of an inner chamber. Arabella, his poor *inamorata*, had no choice but to follow the man she loved into the darkness, and did just that.

"I'm not in the least tired!" Emma proclaimed to Simon, whom she interrupted in the midst of a yawn. "And I am going for a walk. Will you escort me, Simon?"

His grudging yes was word enough for Emma, who preceded him in jumping up and running out into the perfume of an early summer afternoon.

Emma, light-headed less from the cider than from the panorama which stretched before her, longed to be at once a part of the scene. The sounds around her, from the songs of the birds and the croon of the breeze, to the enchanting melody of the stream that flowed past the inn and away among the meadows, sounded only joy in her ears.

"Come, Simon, let us follow this gentle brook," she encouraged him and immediately set out down the flower-filled banks. "Oh, look!" she cried as she indicated something in the distance. "See where the stream broadens

. . . I believe I see a small boat floating among the lily pads. And, oh, regard that fetching little footbridge!''

Although he seemed to draw so much of his inspiration from nature, Simon would never name his happiest moments from among those endured outdoors. The brooks of his mind contained no worms or mud, and the tempests of his imaginings were easily contained. Outside, he grumbled to himself, any horror might be lurking in the underbrush, or even among those silly flowers (which themselves made him sneeze). Briefly he contemplated the fearsome prospect that married life with Emma might take place largely on foot, with Simon's being led a merry chase out of doors and across the globe.

"Simon! Do not dally!" Emma urged him. "Isn't this a paradise?''

"Umm," Simon muttered, preoccupied with the task of protecting his new and expensive trousers from the dirt of the path.

Squinting her eyes against the blinding sunlight and her lack of spectacles, Emma observed a speck on the distant footbridge, which she took to be a human form.

"Look! There's somebody on the footbridge! Perhaps it's one of the other guests. Let's say hello!" she cried with renewed enthusiasm, and off she scurried, feeling, momentarily, a great affection for the entire universe.

"Hallo!" she caroled when she was near enough to ascertain that the form on the bridge was female.

"Hallo," floated back the answer, amiable but indistinct over the rush of the brook.

Waving her hand in greeting, Emma tripped daintily toward the figure on the bridge, motioning Simon eagerly to follow.

"Darling, we have visitors," the woman shouted to a personage presently lost to view. Immediately a man emerged from a side path to join her, bearing a bouquet of freshly picked flowers.

Abruptly Emma felt Simon freeze behind her and was pondering the cause, when her steps took her near enough to recognize the couple who waited together on the bridge. By then it was too late, for the lady of the pair was presently calling, "Emma! Emma Davenant, how you've changed!" Florissa de Coucy came clearly into view, smiling as she graciously accepted the flowers from Marcus Leicester's arms into her own.

It was shock alone that enabled Emma, almost unawares, to set her foot upon the bridge, to stroll gracefully toward the waiting couple, and even to return a cousinly peck to the evil Delilah's roseate cheek.

"Emma! Dear little Emma!" cooed the belle, holding the little cousin at arm's length to garner a portraitist's view. "And," Florissa continued, her eyes shifting to the next surprise, "can that be Simon? Simon Herbert? Can it be?" And with that, she made to greet her former fiancé. Florissa's withdrawal to admit the newest player to their little stage left Emma briefly alone in Marcus's company.

Employing the moment to best advantage, she hissed, "How much does she know?"

He answered quietly. "Of our association? Nothing. Nothing at all."

"And I trust she will not," Emma concluded, a pleasant and distant smile cloaking the urgency of her words.

"Lady Emma—" Marcus began, but before he could continue, Emma interrupted him.

"You have received my letter?" she inquired coldly.

"Lady Emma," he began, an undeniable agitation in his voice. "Lady Emma," he repeated unhappily, but just then Florissa and Simon, past differences apparently happily resolved, arrived to join them.

Perceiving her cousin and her fiancé in mutual silence,

156

Florissa set about to remedy that state. "Have you two introduced yourselves? No? Emma Davenant, my dear little cousin, this is Marcus Leicester." Her smile was clearly intended to bless their meeting.

"We are acquainted, Florissa," Marcus replied tersely.

"And Simon as well?" she pursued. When Marcus indicated he and the poet had met, Florissa drawled, "Oh yes, of course. You would all know each other. London is such a small village after the Continent!"

For one interminable moment, the four figures froze into silence once more, but they were rescued from this new awkwardness by Simon who, in a rare moment of grace, lightly suggested, "I say, don't you think we should be returning?"

"But of course," Florissa cooed, grabbing Emma's hand as they set off, daintily tripping down a path abloom with primrose.

Somehow the unlikely foursome wended its way back to the inn. So deeply distressed had our heroine become that she was all but unaware of their progress, and of the utter silence of Marcus and Simon, who followed in the ladies' wake.

Meanwhile Florissa chattered on. "Emma, dear, I am so enamored of your new coiffure! I'm dying to try it! Perhaps it is a bit too . . . *gamin*, too . . . boyish, but, still, it is so . . . refreshing."

Florissa's coiffure, on the other hand, was elaborately set off with various flowers and pouffs and even a ribbon or two, and her blue beribboned muslin frock disclosed as much as muslin possibly could.

"And your frock," the belle continued. "Such a triumph of simplicity, yet how daring. For one with a figure as . . . *slender* as yours . . . to display it so generously." This was accompanied by a perceptible swelling of the speaker's own ample *décolletage*, as she continued. "And see how sweet you can look, once you get a bit of country color into those sallow London cheeks!" Abruptly dismissing her interlocutor, Florissa turned her well-dressed head to exclaim to the gentlemen, "Is this not the most extraordinary of coincidences? That such dear old friends' paths should cross on a footbridge in Devon! Is it not fabulous?"

Simon's only response was to stumble over a rock, Marcus's to restrain the fall. Turning back to her newfound relation, Florissa again sounded her wonder at the pastoral occurrence, then inquired, "But how came you to know of this place?"

To which, Emma heard another Emma reply clearly, "It was Lord Leicester who first told me of it, some weeks ago."

"Amazing!" mused Florissa, and smoothly continued. "How much it pleases me, dear Emma, that you and Marcus seem to be friends. Is he not the most divine of men? And his way with women . . . so gallant. I have always maintained that Marcus Leicester can make a frump feel beautiful as a belle!"

Before Florissa could pursue any further her present perilous course, Marcus had adeptly grabbed her arm and firmly maneuvered her ahead on the path. Hence, Emma was left to the protection of her befuddled suitor, and to the prospect of a future as disappointing as the past.

A mauve and orchid sunset glowed in the French windows of the charming chamber, but its serene beauty went unnoticed by our downcast heroine.

Immediately upon the party's return to the inn, Emma, pleading indisposition, had repaired to her rooms for a rest, past caring what the others said, or what they might make of the current goings-on. She paused briefly to examine her appearance in a sitting room mirror. Alas her quiet charms were quite outfaced by the dazzling image of Florissa. That further dissatisfaction sent her directly to lie down, Barnaby at her side, with the twin pains of humiliation and disappointment coming upon her in waves like a megrim.

"Oh, Barnaby," she cried. "Now I have gotten what I want, and I am not one whit happier than I was before I had it. At last I am assured of Simon's devotion—"

Her words were interrupted by a deep-throated growl. "I know you don't like him, but you'll grow to like him." The growl increased in intensity. "Well, perhaps you'll adjust to him." A dubious growl resounded. "Oh, I know your objections. He is not as generous as . . . say . . . Lord Leicester," (the growling here diminished but recommenced as she went on) "nor as compassionate . . . nor as gracious as that person . . . but he is much more . . . *exciting*! Artistic! Passionate." The growls reached a fevered pitch. "Oh, what does it matter, anyway," she continued, "what Marcus is or isn't? He is of no further interest to me. He has finished his required work, and I feel sure he is as relieved as I to be allowed the privacy of his own life once more." But this provoked in her a flood of the most happy memories of her instruction, which brought down her spirits even more.

"Oh, Barnaby," she moaned, "how could he have allowed this to occur? How could he humiliate me so? Of course, I can't blame him for preferring her. She is ravishing, even more ravishing than before." At that, Barnaby growled again. "Oh, I appreciate your dislike of her. And I compliment you on chasing her around the room when she called you 'kitty,' but, even so, you must admit she is a most glorious creature." Barnaby's further disapproval was interrupted by a knock at the door. In answer to Emma's query, the low-pitched response was, "Marcus."

"Marcus?" she called, stricken.

159

"Yes; may I speak with you, Lady Emma? Florissa and I depart as soon as she and her maid finish packing, and I very much desire a word with you. For only a moment. May I come in?"

Steeling herself and conquering the tremble in her voice, Emma proudly announced, "Certainly not, Lord Leicester."

"But I must speak with you," he insisted.

"Lord Leicester? You forget your manners. For one thing, I am indisposed. For another, respectable ladies do not admit gentlemen to their boudoirs." So firm was her tone, he never could have suspected the tears running down her cheeks.

"But—"

"I am sorry, Lord Leicester. It is quite impossible. We shall have occasion to meet in London. Shall we not meet Thursday next at the masquerade?"

"Yes, we shall." Marcus's final words carried with them a sudden and baffling hint of anticipation. "Yes, we shall assuredly meet at the masquerade!"

Chapter XXII

RARELY HAD A night been so perfect for a masquerade beneath the stars. To be sure, the mysterious lady strolling with her two masked escorts down a maze near the bandstand had never moved with more grace or shone with more delicate charm. Beneath the flowing ebony cape she wore a dazzling gown of black muslin which clung provocatively to her slim figure; sleeveless, its bodice plunged low and rose again toward the creamy shoulders. Black elbow gloves graced her bare arms; upon her feet were the finest black satin sandals.

The eyes that twinkled through the holes in the mask she held to her face were green as the sea, giving the finishing touch to the mask itself: a full face of elegant mien, formed of unadorned white silk over cambric. At first glance, it seemed to glow with the perfect yet abstract female beauty of a classical statue. Only to an attentive observer would the idealized features begin to take on a slight familiarity; finally one might recognize the face of Emma Davenant as envisioned by a man who loved her.

Emma herself, however, was at a loss to guess who the mask was supposed to represent, or why Marcus had chosen it for her. Nor did she care to pursue a train of thought that might lead to her tutor. By the end of the evening she would have given her promise to Simon, the man she had so long desired, and her course of study would in any case have been brought to the happiest of conclusions.

Still, from moment to moment, amidst the mazes and glowing lights and music, Emma was forced to hold back the tears which threatened to overwhelm her again. Had she been any less the admiral's daughter, she might have forestalled what promised to be an unavoidable new encounter with Marcus. Being the woman she was, she determined instead to confront him, and his vile fiancée, whilst securing a man of her own.

"I think I'd like a blueberry ratafia," Emma informed her gallant companions.

At once, both Simon and Anthony Chase snapped to attention. Chase was done up in plum satin, brown velvet, gold silk, and a clown's mask with a red nose. Simon, as was his wont, wore black; the crimson lining of his cape blazed below his Mephistophelian mask.

"Stay right there, Emma!" Simon called, as he raced toward the pavilion, hoping to outfare Sir Anthony in the satisfaction of his mistress's desire.

"Yes, do!" echoed Sir Anthony, as he, too, sped toward the pavilion.

Left alone to muse, Emma was, despite the cares of the recent past, forced to admire the radiant scene about her. An emerald carpet of lush grass led the masqued strollers to the Grand Pavilion, sparkling with the diamond blue of moonlight in the distance. The verdant alley featured parallel paths, fashioned to allow a man and a maid to stroll together toward the bandstand. These lovers' lanes were guarded by towering hedges of deepest green, manicured in fanciful designs and strung with lanterns strategically placed to hint at the existence of secret nooks camouflaged by the overbrush.

Every now and then, a masked and giggling couple emerged from behind the hedge, having arrived back to civilization after being delightfully lost in the forests of Vauxhall.

The night was wonderfully mild, and the music most rapturous. Here, in solitude, Emma could feel her spirits rising to meet the gaiety of the occasion. Here, before the night was over, she would pledge herself to the man she had long sought.

Suddenly, a figure appeared and came rushing toward her from the direction of the pavilion, calling, ''Emma? Emma, is that you?'' And, to Emma's dismay, Florissa de Coucy stood before her.

''Aha! I recognized your mask, dear Emma!'' Florissa chirped. ''I forced Marcus to describe it to me!''

''Florissa!'' Emma could only murmur, struck as she was by the dazzling silver-gowned form before her. Florissa's coiffure was studded with gleaming moonbeams, stars, planets, and constellations of the brightest diamonds. Beneath the heavenly hair, Florissa displayed the full-faced mask of a silver fox, with eyes, however, of an unusual violet blue. The excellent pelt of that very animal narrowly bordered the hood and hem of a gray velvet domino which itself was embroidered in silver.

''Florissa,'' Emma smiled bravely beneath the refuge of her mask, ''are you not warm in all that fur and velvet?''

''Warm?'' warbled the indomitable belle. ''Not in the least! Do silver foxes not wear fur in the springtime?''

Not at the Vauxhall Gardens, Emma was tempted to reply, but held her tongue.

"Have you seen Marcus?" Florissa inquired, leading her cousin to a bench and inviting her to sit for a moment.

"No," Emma replied. "Have you lost him?"

"I may have. We were separated near the bandstand, when I was swept up with the crowd and carried in this direction," she sighed, then continued. "You know, Emma, I am not enjoying myself in the least. Since Marcus made me promise to reveal my presence here to no one, I must do without company . . ."

Was this, Emma wondered, the first time Florissa had ever found herself alone? But her musings on this point were cut off by Florissa's continued babble. "Really, Emma, I don't know what has become of Marcus since last we met. He seems so . . . changed . . . so reticent . . . I might almost suspect he had undertaken and failed with one of his lost causes. Poor Marcus! He wants to make the whole world happy and is so crushed when he does not succeed! You know, Emma, he comes to my lodgings only to play the part of Hamlet—all moody and indecisive. He provides absolutely no entertainment whatever. I think I *must* get him out of dreary old England at the first opportunity!"

Emma, freshly angered by the possibility of Marcus's pity, concurred, "Yes. London grows very stale. But for now, until you find Lord Leicester, you may stroll with Anthony Chase and Simon and me. The gentlemen will any moment be returning from the pavilion, and then we can set off."

"Yes, I suppose so." Florissa examined the notion, then was struck by a sudden thought. "By the way, Emma, that Anthony Chase . . . He is wealthy, is he not?"

"Massively," responded Emma, surprised at the wandering eye of Marcus's fiancée.

"Hm. Yes, I thought so. Yes, I'll join you," Florissa decided just as a male form appeared and paused before the seated demoiselles, forcing them to raise their masks to their faces.

"Good evening, ladies," the masked visitor offered in a leonine voice instantly familiar to Emma. But from where, she could not recall. Florissa, however, leaped to her feet to return the greeting.

"Oh, sir, your lion's mask proclaims, rather than disguises, your identity, Lord Wellington," Florissa cooed.

The great hero, flattered but a bit crestfallen at having been found out, inquired of the silver beauty, "Have we met before?"

"Ah yes, dear sir," Florissa fixed him with an alluring glance. "But perhaps I should not tell you where, lest I disclose my identity."

Emma, not in the least surprised by her sudden invisibility, was surprised when Wellington, rather than urging Florissa on, turned to her. "And you, o lady of classic countenance, have we, too, met before?"

Behind the mask, Emma's lips turned upward in a little smirk, but to the august personage her face still shone forth with Grecian mystery.

"Dear lady, you demur? Will you not speak? Are you afraid your dulcet tones will all too readily give you away?"

Emma, in fact, had no particular notion of why she had not spoken, but instinct advised reticence and she obeyed.

Again Florissa broke in. "You must forgive my friend, Lord Wellington. She is a bit . . . provincial . . . a little overawed." But her attempt to turn Wellington's attention back to her was unsuccessful, for he replied, "I must strenuously disagree. This lovely lady's costume and her presence display a grace and a serenity equaled only in Lord Elgin's 'marbles.' "

At last Emma deigned to lift her glance to meet the hero's own. "Your gaze, madame," he murmured, "is of truly amazing clarity. I feel it sees at once through my hero's guise to the simple heart beating beneath. Perhaps you are truly the goddess your costume suggests."

As Florissa nearly pawed the earth with her silver slipper, Emma held her penetrating gaze, and her silence.

"Those eyes!" Wellington's contemplation was broken off as he exclaimed, "Those clear, green eyes! Aha! I have recalled you! At Mrs. Fitzherbert's table. You are that enchanting conversationalist next to whom I sat. Admit it! Are you not Marcus Leicester's fiancée?"

"*I* am Marcus Leicester's fiancée!" interjected a distressed Florissa. "*She* is not."

Wellington turned on the belle a look of the sort reserved for inmates at Bedlam, then persisted, "Admit it! You are Lady Emma Davenant!"

"Emma Davenant is not Marcus Leicester's fiancée!" Florissa continued to insist to the air, as Emma reluctantly consented to nod in affirmation.

"It is indeed a pleasure to meet again, my lady." He gently took her hand and brought it to his lips. "I live in the hope that soon we shall dine together again." Then he gallantly took his leave, his path crossing that of the two returning swains. They discovered a pair of ladies where there had been only one, and found both strangely quiet, their masks, however, betraying not so much as a hint of the moods they happily concealed. As it happened, Florissa's features were unattractively screwed up with rage, while Emma smiled almost too contentedly, happily recalling the maxim that silence is golden.

Chapter XXIII

SIR ANTHONY, HAVING been maneuvered by Florissa a distance away down the path toward the pavilion, Simon took Emma's hand in his and walked her slowly toward a particularly fetching grotto.

"My dearest Emma, our companions will all too soon be looking for us, so I must speak quickly. There is an issue of utmost importance which I desire more than anything to discuss with you."

"Yes?" She looked up at him modestly, allowing him to capture her other hand as well.

"This is my plan," the poet began. "I am going to announce to our party that I must depart briefly to pay a gambling debt to a fella I'd arranged to meet here. I will away to complete my errand, at which time I will inform your friends that you are taking a stroll alone. Once you have secured your freedom, search out the Nereid Fountain which lies on the other side of the gardens. Just follow that path there, and you'll arrive directly. I'll be waiting for you as the clock strikes one. Now, quickly, before they return. In fifteen minutes, then,'' and he fled, blowing her a kiss.

Once alone, Emma, masked and myopic, ambled at a leisurely pace, breathing in the wonder and mystery of this paradisiacal garden of scandalous delights. Maze encountered maze, some illumined by candles, others dark enough for the most intimate confidences. On the air floated the perfume of pleasure. The wind carried to her the laughter of the crowd and the music. So divine was the night, so diverting the scene, that for moments she was almost able to forget the events of the past day. Only once did the tears actually prick the corners of her eyes; only a single tear escaped to roll down her cheek.

She proceeded along a particularly serpentine path, enjoying the perfume of flowers. Suddenly she heard something behind her. Whirling around, she thought she saw a figure disappearing through a break in the maze, then realized it must have been a lover who had lost his way. She continued on her solitary way to her destination.

As she followed the curving path, the Nereid Fountain rose up before her. An oratorio of a fountain it was, gleaming against the night sky in the illumination of stars and lanterns and moonlight and candles.

The ebony marble sprites and cupids sailed on the backs of huge gold porpoises, and the company bore on their assembled backs the vessel on which stood the ebony form of the Queen of the Nereids. Her lithe marble form was of porcelainlike delicacy, and she was clad in the most fragile of golden raimants. She held aloft a gold crown to bless the crystalline sprays which played about her.

At that moment the sound of fireworks filled the air, and great constellations of color turned against the sky. It was one o'clock.

"Emma!" Had she heard her name? Certainly not. Then it came again. "Emma!" More insistently. "I'm over here, in the bushes."

It was assuredly Simon, but why was he hiding? Of course, within the cover of the hedges, Sir Anthony would never discover them.

"Where are you?" she called softly.

"Here! Right here!" And, as if to guide her steps, the hedges rustled.

Blindly following the rustling through the absolute darkness, Emma found herself caught in dense foliage, where no light penetrated. "Where are you?" she whispered again, more urgently, attempting to fend off the overhanging branches.

"I'm right here," came the reply. "Don't move. I'm about to take your hand." Suddenly an unseen hand grasped hers.

"Come over here!" Emma ordered, uncertain as to where "here" was.

"Not until you consent to be my wife!" She could hear his other hand pushing through the bushes to reach hers. His voice was muffled by the whispering of leaves as he attempted to move. "Give me your word now! I can wait no longer!"

And without a moment's hesitation, she bravely replied, "Yes."

"Yes?" The muffled voice sounded resonant with joy.

"Yes," she repeated, surprised by the sinking sensation accompanying her answer. "Yes, you have my word!"

And just as the other hand completed its tour through the leaves to locate hers and draw her closer, she heard a voice from the path calling, "Emma!"

"Simon!" she whispered to the formless figure somewhere near her. "Someone is calling me! Perhaps it's Sir Anthony. Let's tell him the good news immediately."

169

"No!" the voice declared. "Not yet!"

"Simon! Don't be silly," she scolded and turned to make her way through the foliage back to the path. "Hallo!" she called to the waiting figure in the distance.

"Emma? What are you doing in the hedge?" the figure shouted. Only as she approached did she realize to her horror that the speaker bore not the foolish face of a clown, but the angry demeanor of the devil.

"Simon! How can it be you? I just—" And she whirled back in the direction whence she had come in time to see, appearing through the underbrush, none other than the masked but still unmistakable Marcus Leicester.

"Lord Leicester!" she shrieked, fighting valiantly to keep herself from falling into a swoon.

"Lord Leicester!" the poet echoed her terrible cry.

"Your humble servant," he drawled. Bowing politely, as if he had just arrived in a drawing room, Marcus brushed the leaves from the shoulders of his dinner jacket. "Thought these things only shed in the fall."

"Lord Leicester!" Emma was beside herself with rage. "How dare you talk of leaves at a time like this?"

"How dare you!" Again the poetic echo sounded.

"You are right, Lady Emma." The scoundrel simply smiled. "Silly to talk of leaves when we have so much else to talk of," and he made to take her hand. Before he could grasp any part of her at all, Emma had wheeled about and taken the arm of the astonished Simon.

"Much to talk of, indeed!" Dragging Simon along, she proceeded briskly down the path back toward the pavilion.

"Come, Simon," she urged. "Faster."

"Certainly, Emma," agreed Simon, deciding to follow Emma's lead and ignore the gentleman trailing closely behind them.

"Let me but remind you, Lady Emma," that person now announced, "you gave me your word."

170

Without turning her head or slowing her pace, Emma retorted, ''My *word* was obtained under false pretenses.''

Again the voice countered, ''I never said I was Simon.''

''He's after your money, Emma,'' Simon contributed to the debate.

''Nonsense, Lady Emma,'' came the retort from behind, ''I must confess many things to you, and the very first is that I am extremely wealthy and don't need your money.''

''A likely tale,'' she shot back, still without inclining her head or dallying.

''If you don't believe me, ask your father.''

''My father? What has my father to do with this?''

''Lady Emma, what your father asked of me I undertook as a *favor*. But, in the process, well . . . that's for later, but for now you need have no concern that I seek your fortune.''

''And what of your . . . fiancée?'' Emma sneered. ''What will Florissa say when she hears you are pledged to me?''

''Lady Emma,'' Marcus announced, his tone now stern. ''If you do not turn around and face me, I will hurry back to the pavilion by a route known only to me and, before you can stop me, will announce our impending marriage to all your friends!''

''No!'' she screamed, shock spinning her around as anger could not. ''No! Please!''

''Then you must speak to me. Now,'' he insisted, apparently caring nothing for the unhappy witness to this encounter.

''All right,'' Emma capitulated. Then, turning to the poet, she suggested, ''Simon, I shall meet you back at the pavilion when we have righted this most embarrassing error. And do not breathe a word to anyone!''

''No . . . no, of course not,'' the suitor stuttered; then, clearly relieved to be liberated, he ran straight away.

"Shall we sit?" Marcus indicated a circular grotto in which was set a small Italianate fountain and several benches.

"No, I'd rather stand," countered Emma, refusing to budge from the path. "Now, what of Florissa?"

"Will you not be seated?" he encouraged her.

"Not only would I prefer not to sit, but I would likewise prefer that you not evade my questions with your infernal courtesy." Emma stood, the features of her unlowered mask coldly staring down upon him.

"All right, as you will . . . Lady Emma. I am loath to talk of Florissa for I am distressed by the fact that by deserting her I have not behaved like a gentleman. In my own defense, I must say that I have tried, in the last few days, to make clear to her as gently as possible my changed intentions. I have even suggested that, since we were never announced, she would suffer no embarrassment. But try as I did, she would not listen."

"I am already somewhat confused by your tale, Lord Leicester," Emma commented curtly.

"Let me, then, return to the beginning. Florissa and I kept company several years ago in Vienna. But our relationship was interrupted by my reluctance to set a date for our marriage and her subsequent return to London and thence again to the Continent. As I was engaged on my solitary travels, Florissa and Lord Jason had struck up an acquaintance, based largely on their mutual desire for wealth, but, having discovered that her penury quite matched his, Simon, disgruntled, returned to England.

"Upon my own return, in fact, the very day we met, I received a letter from Florissa urging me to consider the resumption of our relationship. She seemed so desperate that I could not deny her the opportunity to journey to England for further discussion."

"And then?" Emma persisted.

"And then, well, you and I grew to know one another, and I began to doubt the wisdom of my invitation to Florissa. By the afternoon of my subsequent disappearance, I had resolved my conflict and begun a letter, advising her of my altered intentions. But just as I had sat down to compose it, a note arrived from Florissa herself, announcing her premature arrival. Off I rushed to her, leaving behind the letter which I had just begun."

"And when you saw her?"

"Ah, when I saw her," he bemoaned the recollection. "Believe me, it was the most unpleasant of surprises to find her expectations so assured. Immediately observing her . . . zest . . . for our impending marriage, I knew I must spirit her out of London before needless mischief was done. Hence, our presence at the inn."

"I see." Her voice, however, promised nothing.

"In all honesty, Lady Emma, my time with Florissa was spent largely in thinking of you. And when you actually appeared, I had made my decision for better or worse." The Beau appeared to have concluded his speech.

"Why didn't you approach me, then?" Emma persisted. So caught up in these revelations was she that only vaguely did she realize they were now strolling down the path toward the pavilion. "Why did you not confess this at the inn?"

"As you will recall, Lady Emma," he responded, stifling a chuckle, "I attempted just that, but you refused to speak to me. As I am certain you would have tonight, had I not resorted to . . . rather desperate . . . measures."

"And how do you plan to inform Florissa of all this?" Emma asked warily.

"She will just now be receiving a note I arranged to be sent to her at the pavilion. In it, I attempted to explain myself and my actions, including my . . . anticipated deception of you here tonight. Admitting that my actions were those of a cad, I nonetheless felt I had to inform her of them before the fact so that she would not be publicly shocked."

"She is reading this missive even now?" Emma gasped.

"Even now," he responded.

"Lord Leicester," Emma asked him deliberately, "were you the figure I saw fleeing into the darkness behind me?"

"I must confess," he replied with a sheepish shrug of the shoulders, "that I have been keeping closer to you than you know. How else would I have beaten Simon to the Nereid Fountain?"

A contemplative silence fell upon them; but as the sparkling lights of the pavilion came into view directly ahead, Emma could restrain herself no longer.

"You have not behaved like a gentleman, sir," she intoned solemnly, glad for the fact that he could not see the delight beneath the goddesslike serenity of her mask.

"Not behaved like a gentleman?" The strain was evident in his eyes, and he seemed barely to notice that they had entered the glittering throng. "Not behaved like a gentleman!" Grasping her arm fiercely, he stopped her in her tracks as he continued. "Madame, I have dissembled, cheated, played the fool, lied to my servants, suffered the company of that insufferable bore Simon, and in addition have had to endure your disdain and the constant torment of my own conscience, all for your love!"

"And do you suppose," she pursued, "that any of that excuses your odious behavior?"

"Odious behavior!" Without warning, he had roughly flung away her arm and begun to shout. "Odious behavior? Just what is it you want of me, madame?" He froze for a moment, then shook his head as if he were coming round following a seizure. "Oh, my God," he cried as his eyes widened in horror. "You have made me shout! In

174

public!'' His rushing sense of shame could not prevent his astonishment on seeing that tears gleamed in her eyes.

"Marcus," she murmured, her voice breaking, "you shouted at me! You do love me!"

"I fail to see the connection, Emma," Marcus replied sternly, nevertheless taking advantage of her vulnerable state to grasp the hand that held the mask and draw it away, revealing her own radiant face.

"Marcus," she smiled at him through her tears, "I wanted proof of your passion. And at last, you have given it to me. You *are* a passionate man, as well as a perfect one."

Now it was his turn to color as they walked together to the table, their hands tightly clasped.

Awaiting the happy couple at the table were an ardent Arabella, masked as the sun, and Harry, garbed as a dark Mongol conquerer. Florissa, having wasted no time, was energetically inveigling Sir Anthony Chase, who sat close to her, in love again. Simon sat alone, brooding deeply. Alas! Gone was the fortune that only moments ago had been within his grasp, gone the luxury and ease that would never be a poet's lot.

Just at that moment a young girl costumed as a milk maid appeared and ran to Arabella's side, demanding, in a whisper, "Is that him? Is that Lord Jason?" Before her sister could respond, Caroline Portney had turned her inquisition on the subject himself. "Are you?" she inquired heatedly, "are you the author of *The Idylls of Sir Percival*?"

Bowing low and removing his mask, the better to present his most romantic smile, Simon modestly admitted that he was indeed the man she sought.

"All the girls in my circle have read your book, and now the boys are, too. Come join my friends over there!" Caroline urged him, and she grabbed his hand and pulled him off to be celebrated.

Emma and Marcus, standing entranced and oblivious to the others, were startled to hear a familiar voice calling, "Yo' heave ho!" And lo and behold, who should appear but the jolly figure of Admiral Davenant masked as a buccaneer, accompanied by a most handsome woman of a certain age in a blue silk domino.

The admiral approached the astonished couple and, after kissing his daughter and shaking Marcus's hand, he introduced the lady on his arm. "And this, my children, is an old friend of mine, Germaine de Staël."

The gracious lady greeted them most warmly, and then inquired, "And when is the wedding to be?"

"The wedding?" Emma stepped back. "How could you have known?"

Her confusion was shared by Marcus. "Yes, we've only just found out ourselves."

"But, William," the lady cried, turning a quizzical glance upon her grinning companion, "you wrote me a month ago that Emma and Lord Leicester were to be wed."

Admiral Davenant, seeing it was too late further to dissemble, simply shrugged his shoulders and looked away sheepishly.

"Father!" Emma would brook no evasion. "Father, how did you know? Unless . . . unless . . ."

And as she and Marcus looked in bewilderment at one another, they arrived at the truth in an instant and burst into laughter.

"Sir, you are a pirate, if I may say so."

"Indeed you may," the admiral allowed. "A pirate who loves his daughter enough to beg, borrow, and steal the only birthday present in Christendom good enough for her. And, by the way, Lieutenant, you might just grant an old man the courtesy of asking for his daughter's hand."

Marcus hastened to correct the grievous error. "Sir, please excuse me, am I granted permission to—?"

"Enough, boy!" the admiral jauntily interrupted. "Do you love Emma?"

"Yes, sir, with all my heart."

"And would you like to kiss her to seal your troth?"

"Yes, sir, with all my heart."

"Emma," her father called his starry-eyed daughter to attention, "what is your desire?"

"Anything that pleases you, Father," she responded with a distinct twinkle.

"Then get on with it and meet us at the bandstand when it's done with." Motioning the group at the table to rise, Admiral Davenant, smiling broadly, marched the jolly band away.

The lovers drew as close as their hearts, and their lips met . . . and after a long and blissful kiss, they linked arms once more and strolled happily off into a passionate future.

And afterward . . .

EMMA TAUGHT MARCUS to argue, and Marcus taught Emma to share . . .

Florissa, having fallen in love at first sight of Sir Anthony's fortune, consented to be wed wealthily, insuring, thereby, that she would be lavishly overdressed 'til the end of her days . . .

Lord Jason soon learned that the love of one woman was less to his taste than the love of a multitude, and became very famous . . .

Young Caroline Portney grew up the following year and became as optimistic as her sister Arabella, who achieved her Harry, and cheerfully continued to delude herself that her husband's black belligerence was manly courage . . .

* * *

And, miracle of miracles, one summer day there appeared in the kitchen of Belgrave Square a small but fiesty female cat, who instantly commanded Barnaby's respect by growling back at him. Realizing he had met his match, Barnaby at once capitulated and began to purr. This advent was considered to be an act of God by Emma and the great cat himself. Only Marcus and the reader know different.

Chasing Rainbows

A novel of love, enduring courage and soaring triumph!

BY
ESTHER SAGER

They grew up on a lush estate in Virginia—Winna, the selfish blonde beauty, and Libby, the lovable auburn-haired lass. Then, at ten, an accident left Libby to face life against towering odds. Yet Libby is a survivor, and it is she who captures the heart of sophisticated Adam Bainbridge.

Suddenly Winna invades their perfect world—with malice and betrayal in her heart. Libby and Adam must learn that love is, like a rainbow, so very hard to catch and keep.

_____ 05849-1 CHASING RAINBOWS $2.95